I0663084

What they have said about the
SHORT STORIES
of Daniel Hoyt Daniels

I loved your stories -- they are delightful, especially the surprise endings. They are even better than O Henry and Maupaussant. I read all thirty of them in two days; I couldn't stop myself.
> -- Maria Atansov, Hilton Head, SC

Well done.
> – Jack Harris, Sarasota, FL

Poignant; touched my heart.
> -- Suzanne Brailey, Gloucester, MA

Extremely creative.
> -- Evelyn Harris, Lincoln, MA

Your tongue in cheek is indeed producing chuckles here. A great job.
> -- Capt. Giles Kelly, USNR, Ret, Washington, DC

Your stories delight me. Your characters are so funny.
> -- Suzy Wolf, Beaufort, SC

We liked your stories.
> -- Ed Wendell, Orange, VA

They all simply flow so beautifully.
> – Nancy Parten, Monroe, NY

As though he were in the room, telling the story.
> – Anne Harris, Sarasota, FL

We loved "Happy Thanksgiving" greatly. We were both very moved. You are a really great writer; I mean that. I shall Xerox it and send it to my children. This story is marvelous.
> -- Frances Huxley, Playwright, Concord, MA

What they have said about the
SHORT STORIES
of Daniel Hoyt Daniels

I liked the prose style – easy to read, and the plots evolved smoothly. The use of words was carefully chosen and concise. The variety made each one stand out by itself. I especially enjoyed reading Baked Alaska, You Took the Words, My Brother-in-Law Is a Jerk, and A Few More Days. Each touched me in a different way. Marie in A Few More Days is a wonderful character. On finishing each of these stories, I had a warm feeling.

Your bitterness in the war stories did not surprise me. The tragic ending of each of them made me think and feel the pain of the protagonists. They were extremely well written.
> -- The Hon. Irving Tragen, former US Ambassador Panama, La Jolla, CA

Quite a few chuckles. You write very well and get the reader's attention right away, and your endings are wonderful. You are also able to write from a woman's point of view, like in "A New Start." "The Rabbit" is great! Reminds me of my time in South Carolina when I volunteered in a school there. I really enjoyed reading these stories.
> -- Ingrid Lander, Longmont, CO

Interesting.
> -- Buzz Richards, Falmouth, MA

Your book is delightful. We especially liked "Happy Thanksgiving" and "John Harvard Fantoma." "Bastille Day" has everything: nostalgia, youth, politics, sex, humor, and history.
> -- Miriam Mauzerall, Dobbs Ferry, NY

My guests liked it too.
> -- Tinica Mather, Silver Spring, MD

I like your style.
> -- Nancy Myers, Beaufort, SC

I am savoring your stories   I chuckle to myself every time I think of "My Brother-in-Law is a Jerk." Thank you so much. I have ordered some copies through Amazon for Christmas presents.
> -- Coleman Nee, Yarmouthport, MA

i

What they have said about the
SHORT STORIES
of Daniel Hoyt Daniels

We read your stories with pleasure; we especially liked "Turkey in the Straw,."
-- Henry and Lois Ross, Nokesville, VA

It is as though O Henry himself were with us again. Daniels is a master storyteller. Delightful.
-- Ethard Van Stee, Novelist, Beaufort, SC

Made me laugh aloud. You write beautifully. Very clever endings.
-- Mimi Rankin, Vienna, VA

A wonderful collection of stories. You are a wonderful writer. "The Live Oak" is my favorite; it made me cry. Also "Hypocrisy" and "Bastille Day."   "You Took the Words" was lots of fun.
-- Nancy Shaw, Summerfield, FL, formerly Beaufort,SC

We like your stories.   You are a natural writer.   We took turns reading them at La Posada Inn..
-- John Snyder, Laredo, TX

I'm enjoying one at a time.
-- Judy Osborne, Boston, MA

Enjoying your book of stories. Appealing style. I like the fact that each can be enjoyed in a short time. Just right when there's a minute or two when one wants to be productive.
-- John Trask, Beaufort, SC

Très bonne humour. Amusing and philosophical at the same time.
-- Michele Wernert-Piper, New York, NY

You are a gifted writer.
-- Mr. and M rs. Francis Williamson, Beaufort, SC

Entertaining and thought-provoking; you are a word-master; sounds so real and true; a treasure.
-- Peg Flanagan, Beaufort, SC

SHORT STORIES
ENCORE

by

DANIEL HOYT DANIELS

author of

"BAKED ALASKA
AND OTHER
SHORT SHORT STORIES"

with
Whimsy, Humor, and Tongue-in-Cheek
for your
Guestroom Bedside Table

All rights reserved, which include the right to reproduce this book or portions thereof in any form except provided by the U.S. Copyright Laws.

Tradepaper Edition 10-digit ISBN: **1-58218-878-5**
Tradepaper Edition 13 digit ISBN: **978-1-58218-878-2**

First DSI Printing: **June 2016**

Published by Digital Scanning, Inc. Scituate, MA 02066
781-545-2100
http://www.Digitalscanning.com

Preface to the third collection, "Short Stories Galore"

These little stories are all fictional works originally written for the amusement and pleasure of the author and his friends. Like the stories in my first two published collections, most of them are completely imaginary, although some of them may have originated from a seed of truth. They can usually be read aloud in ten or fifteen minutes, which is the approximate amount of time that used to be allotted to each participant attending the periodic meetings of the Beaufort Writers' Group. Although the Group is no longer active, I must acknowledge the helpful guidance and encouragement I received there, primarily from Ethard Van Stee, the organizer and stylish director of the Group. The stories are all unrelated to one another. If the same name appears in more than one story, it is not to be implied that it is the same character. The stories are not arranged in any particular order, and appear approximately as they were written chronologically.

I have always appreciated comments and suggestions from many various friends, family, colleagues, and acquaintances, who may see themselves in some of my stories whether in the limelight, twilight, or taillight. I shall neither embarrass you nor swell your egos by calling names, but you know who you are... at least some of you do. Thank you.

Any errors are of course my own. Comments on these pieces, or requests for reproduction or other use of them, will be welcomed by the author.

Daniel H. Daniels   or   Daniel H. Daniels
PO Box 1681   PMB 47, Suite B
Beaufort, SC 29901   2724 61st Street
                              Galveston, TX 77551

Preface

People sometimes ask me whether a particular story of mine is true or imaginary. The clever reply is of course, "Yes." However, the answer is that each is a mix of truth and imagination, but rarely in equal proportions. Some are almost complete fabrications with only an occasional touch of truth for flavor. A few may be substantially true with but slight embellishment to help the story flow. It would be difficult to say what proportion of any story is truth. On the one hand, truth may sometimes seem quite far fetched and unbelievable; perhaps, in that case, "truth is stranger than fiction." On the other hand, sometimes good fiction can be made to sound very real; perhaps how real it sounds may be one measure of how good it is.

I like to read stories aloud, and, whether they are truth or fiction, I always try to give them as much verisimilitude as possible. Occasionally, after I have read aloud one of my most preposterous and implausible tales, with a smooth voice and a straight face, one of my listeners, with an equally straight face, will come up to me and ask, "Did that really happen?" I am always delighted.

I hope these stories will delight you too. If any one them does not particularly strike your fancy, go on to the next one. It will be different. They are all designed to be read aloud. Read them aloud to each other after you have gone to bed. If they put you to sleep, there is no harm done.

I always welcome comments and suggestions from my readers.

Finally, once again I want to thank Digital Scanning Inc. and Mr. Brian Shillue for their splendid work in the publication of this book and other works of mine.

Winter   Summer

Daniel Hoyt Daniels   or   Daniel Hoyt Daniels
PMB 47, Suite B   PO Box 42
2724 61st Street   Spencertown, NY 12165
Galveston, TX 77551

                                     danielhdaniels@yahoo.com

Foreword

Welcome to *Short Stories Encore*, the fifth collection of uniquely enticing stories by my friend, Daniel Hoyt Daniels. Since his first batch of delightful characters entered my life in *Baked Alaska*, one or another of his volumes has inevitably been on my bedside table to help ease me into sleep.

I must confess that I am addicted to the array of characters that were conjured in the mind of this 21st century Scheherazade. I am hooked. I usually limit myself to one story a night, my last piece of mental exercise before I turn off the light. I have found the antics of Dan's intriguing characters at times pleasing and at other times horrifying. I have reread certain favorites several times, such as "The Prodigal Calf ", "Getting Even", "Divorce Old French Style", "The Astrologer and the King", "Once a Butler", "The Double Agent", and "My Sister's Butler." When I finish a story, sometimes I ask myself whether Dan drew part of that character from someone I know or even from something I myself said or did.

This array of stories is not what I would have predicted from Daniel Hoyt Daniels. Many years ago, Dan and I worked together in the mundane profession of the American Foreign Service. We were colleagues in the Economic Unit of the US Embassy in Panama. Dan was the prudent and discriminating analyst of complex reports on the Panamanian GNP, national budget, business activity, and trade. His incisive mind, knowledge of history, languages, and skill in his use of words were the trademarks of his work. But, I never suspected that he was also a spinner of yarns -- a gifted storyteller.

So, you can imagine my surprise when I wandered into the igloo of "Baked Alaska" and found an entirely different Daniel Hoyt Daniels -- a colleague who has progressed from dissecting dry economic data to exploring the virtues, vanities, and vulnerabilities of ordinary human beings like you and me.

Dan tells us that his stories are written "with whimsy, humor, and tongue-in-cheek," but they are also insights into our human experience. I suspect that he is constantly appraising and dissecting his everyday experiences and the people who populate them as he imagines their motivation, drive, intention, or inner character. He must constantly be asking himself the five questions of journalism: who, what, why, when, and how. Why are they doing what they are doing? People may not be economic data, but people lend themselves to similar inspection and analysis. Dan has substituted us human beings for economic data, and converted dry analysis into enticing, often compelling, stories of the human experience.

His short stories are wry, often ending with an unexpected twist or perhaps a surprising act of valor or cowardice. When I start reading a tale, I am never sure whether I will close it with a smile, a shudder, or a tear. Dan imbues his people with human traits of kindness or greed, wisdom or folly, respect or envy, grace or malice. You are never sure which until the last line. Each story has its own flavor. One never knows what ironic twist or act of generosity will take shape as the story spins out in each tersely written sentence, paragraph, and page. How he has spun so many stories from his imagination is a reflection of his discerning eye of the society in which we live.

With the experience of the first four collections, I entered with great anticipation into this one, the fifth collection, *Short Stories Encore*. Where will Dan take us this time to meet new friends and face new experiences? Will I meet a new Blanche of Burgundy or another Pomfret Pennypecker Pumpernickel? Will he transport me back to medieval Europe or the Civil War or the Great Depression?

Well, I don't want to spoil your pleasure by telling you my favorites or commenting on the twists and turns that beset a variety of intriguing characters set in the Silicon Valley, Caribbean Islands, suburbia, Fort Donelson, or even Rome, Georgia. Read for yourself and enjoy each incursion into some of the lives of many fascinating people as they engage in noble and illegal pursuits, acts of friendship and betrayal, good and evil.

Again, welcome to *Short Stories Encore*, the fifth collection! Take your time and revel in the feast that Daniel Hoyt Daniels has prepared for us. And, take your time to digest every morsel.

-- Irving G. Tragen
Ambassador of the United States of America (Ret.)

La Jolla, CA
March 28, 2016

SHORT STORIES ENCORE

Page

Virus Infection

"Wow, would you look at that!" said my wife, over the breakfast table the other morning, as we were finishing our coffee. "It sounds almost like another Snowden case."

"Lord Snowdon the Royal lover-boy, or Edward Snowden the whistle-blower?" said I, looking up from the sports page, where I had been checking on the Braves' last game. We'd been out to dinner the previous evening, so I had missed it on TV. (They lost to the Phillies 5-4 after leading for seven innings.)

"I was thinking Snowden the whistle-blower, as you call him, the one who was in the news so much a while ago -- the Snowden guy that leaked all that classified information. This article is about a man who has come out and ratted on his former employers at a big computer company, citing illegal business practices. 'Illegal, unethical, and unscrupulous,' it says. They are calling it the biggest scam since the Teapot Dome. Here, you read it," and she passed the business section back over to me.

Arrant nonsense was my first reaction, but then I read on. It wasn't just any computer company. This gigantic scam operation was being run by the ABC Corp., the American Beauty Computer Corporation, one of the ten fastest-growing high-tech companies in America. Although it was only eight years old, ABC had annual income in the

1

hundreds of millions. I couldn't believe my eyes. I had personal knowledge that this was a fine company; I had been a client of theirs, and they had served me well in the past.

ABC is said to have gotten started, like Apple, in the garage of some computer nerds. The founders, William and Theodore Waterman, were cousins who grew up near each other in Menlo Park, the heart of what is affectionately known as "Silicon Valley." They weren't able to get into Stanford, but took computer courses at the Palo Alto Community College and San Jose State. They got their experience working in computer shops and stores like Best Buy and Staples, which had experts called "geeks" or "nerds" to help customers with their computer problems. They also tinkered in their own time.

Then when they were in their mid-twenties, Bill and Ted decided to strike out on their own. They had some ideas for making money in the computer world, and figured they could make a good bit more than they had been earning as salaried employees. So they founded the ABC Corporation. The main focus of the company derived from certain specialized skills the young men had developed regarding computer viruses. They based the company's operations primarily on purging their customers' computers from the insidious viruses that were so rapidly increasing in numbers and viciousness. Before long they were selling and installing hundreds of anti-virus programs, mostly good for one year, renewable, for a nice fat fee. It was a profitable operation.

The meteoric rise in the ABC Corporation's business activity and in its financial position was recognized throughout the business world. Louis Ruykhauser, of "Wall Street Week," mentioned the company on one of his programs, and Paul Kangas even had the cousins appear on his TV show.

And as I said, I had personal knowledge of the excellent work the ABC could do.

I am not a computer expert myself -- far from it -- but I do use my computer a great deal in my business and in my personal life. I am, in fact, almost computer-illiterate, the same way I am plumbing-illiterate and grass-cutting-illiterate. However, I am personnel-savvy, and I have always been able to find competent people who are able and willing, for a fee, to fill the lacunae and the needs left by my own shortcomings.

Before I learned of the ABC, I caught a nasty and tenacious computer virus. It even had a name, "Trojan Horse," which subtly suggested the deceptive ease with which it could penetrate the inner workings of one's operations. That cost me about $250 and several days wasted time for the period it took my local computer service company to find and clear out the virus.

I sometimes wonder what kind of Machiavellian humor drives the creators of computer viruses. I have been told hackers do it for fun, but that is just someone's supposition. Is it an internal thrill that people get from knowing they are having some effect or influence on the world around them? Do they, like graffiti-painting vandals, get a thrill just from the thought that thousands of people must see or feel the effects of their handiwork? Strange, because, like the bomber pilots over Dresden or Guernica, they don't even to get to enjoy the sight of the devastation and suffering wrought by their endeavors. I have never seen any serious analysis of why people create computer viruses whose damaging effects they can never see or be aware of directly. It would be an interesting study.

Anyway, as I was saying, sometime after my unpleasant experience with the Trojan Horse, my computer caught another virus. This one was simply called "Smiley." How sick, for Smiley was ten times more damaging than Trojan Horse had been, and much more tenacious. Of course, I didn't know its name at first, but Smiley made my computer do all sorts of things it wasn't supposed to do, and blocked it from doing things it *was* supposed to do. It moved my files around; it changed the dates on some of my records; it caused an hour's delay in calling up any file that had been viewed in the past 24 hours; it flashed pictures of weird sci-fi drawings on top of the windows over my screen and my work. It was driving me mad.

I took it to my regular computer shop and left it there for two weeks. I had to buy a new lap-top to handle current matters I was working on, but my regular one, with the virus, had valuable records and information, including my writings and essays and letters and years of material that I could not afford to lose. (I know that once a week I should copy everything that I have on my computer to an external flash drive or thumb drive or something for safe keeping, but I had not done that in a long while. I'll know better next time.) My computer man gave up. "I have never seen anything like this before," he said wearily.

4

I tried the guys at Staples, and then Best Buy, where I had bought the computer in the first place. They were sure they could fix it, they told me, but several days later they acknowledged defeat. "The good news, Sir," they said, "is that we are not going to charge you for the hours -- only for the diagnostic fee of $80."

"Thanks a lot."

I tried one or two other places, all with the same result. "Can't fix it. This is a virus that doesn't respond to any of our standard purging practices. Sorry."

But I wasn't ready to give up. Half of my life and three quarters of my business was right there on that computer. But I did have the new one, practically empty, that I had bought as a temporary substitute -- at least I could write a letter, or see what time it was, or check today's date, or even go back on the Internet, Font of all Knowledge, Source of all Wisdom.

Then I had an idea: Internet!. That's what I should do -- go on the Internet and seek computer advisory services. So that's what I did, and I found a plethora of them, but one in particular caught my eye. Its web site was headed in large, bold, colored, block letters, announcing, "WE SPECIALIZE IN DIFFICULT VIRUS REMOVAL," and then, underneath, in smaller print: "The more difficult it is, the more we like it."

I called the 800 number and got a bright technician with an English accent who lived in Travancore or somewhere. He told me to turn my computer back on and put in a code

5

number, and click on "yes" to authorize him to take over remote control of it. I then watched the screen for five or ten minutes, and saw my cursor jumping around under the guidance of an invisible hand, incomprehensible views of columns and hundreds of lines of meaningless numbers and gibberish. And then a window appeared, saying "Yes, we can fix it. Our service will cost $449.99 and will be guaranteed for one year. If you accept, please enter your sixteen digit credit card number and expiration date (Visa or MasterCard only, no American Express please, sorry) and click on "continue."

What else could I do? $449.99 was a cheap price to pay for half my life and three quarters of my business. So I did it. And right away my computer began to work properly once again. No more virus! I was delighted. Overjoyed. I would have paid double that, I thought to myself. Or triple. That genius! What a splendid company, this ABC! How lucky I was to find them! I must tell my friends; maybe write a letter to the editor of our local newspaper to tell of the joy the ABC Corporation brought back into my life.

* * * * *

So I was appalled the other morning to read that a former ABC employee named Michael Delraton had leaked information to the press condemning ABC's unethical business practices -- ABC, who had been my salvation! I read on: "... has for several years bilked its customers of millions of dollars by providing anti-virus services whose sole purpose was to counter the deleterious effects of viruses that the ABC Corporation itself had created and disseminated into the public domain."

In short, the ABC Corporation was good at removing the Smiley virus because they were the people who had designed it and spread it about in the first place. It was a grand operation and made lots of money, contributing millions of dollars to our nation's GDP -- our Gross Domestic Product -- as well as immeasurable misery to thousands of human beings, including me.

At that point I felt something warm and wet in my lap. At first I didn't know what it was, but then I realized it was only my coffee that I had spilled.

THE END

Hitting for the Circuit

Felipe Manuel Berra was born in the Dominican Republic in 1987. Like many other young boys there, he had a consuming love of baseball. When Felipe was nine years old, his father took him along on a four-day business trip to Tampa. It was early March, and major-league baseball "spring training" was in full swing. On their last day in Florida, his father took him to see the Yankees play the Phillies in a "Grapefruit League" game. It was the most wonderful thing that ever happened to Felipe. Although he had already shown great interest and even some prowess in the sport, after seeing the real Yankees, Felipe could think of almost nothing but baseball. Back in the Dominican Republic he played catch and practiced batting whenever he could, joined every little group or team that he could find, and played regularly throughout his elementary and high-school years. His heroes of course were Alex Rodriguez and Sammy Sosa, fellow Dominicans who had hit (so to speak) the big time, but he had also heard a lot about Mickey Mantle and Yogi Berra (although he was not related to Yogi). That was when he changed his name, his middle name anyway, from Manuel to Mickey. Obviously, he didn't need to change his last name. He was now Felipe Mickey Berra. People sometimes asked if he were related to Yogi Berra. "Maybe distant relatives," answered Felipe rather equivocally, thinking it would be nice if it were true, "but Yogi was from the Missouri branch of the family."

Upon graduation, Felipe was recruited by the Licey Tigers of the Dominican Pro Baseball League (LIDOM), where, over the next three years, he broke several long-standing records for both hitting and fielding, and accordingly came to the attention of the ubiquitous major league scouts. He was good. He thereupon got signed up by the Atlanta Braves and was sent to their Class A farm team in Rome, Georgia (formerly Macon).

At Rome he was a good fielder, but his batting was phenomenal. Not just his batting average, but also his slugging average, which takes into account extra-base hits. He was always eager and energetic. Always on time, or early, for practice, always friendly with the coaches and other players, liked by the fans, willing to accept any assignment, a good team man. But also ambitious and a bit proud. His hitting statistics and on-base records were outstanding. He hit two home runs in each of three different games, and on one especially good day he had three home runs in one game. He was the first player in some years to do that at Rome. Now he had a new target: he wanted to "hit for the circuit," that is, he wanted to have a single, a double, a triple, and a home run, all in one game. Mickey Mantle and Alex Rodriguez and a number of others had done it, but Yogi Berra never. "I'll do it," asserted Felipe (now Mickey), "and I'll dedicate it to Yogi." Twice in his career he had already come close, once with a homer, two doubles and a single, and once with a single, a double, and, would you believe, two triples. What a waste of triples, he thought. You see, triples are the rarest to come by, and are much rarer than homers or doubles. It is unusual indeed for a player to hit two triples in one game -- far less common than two homers.

10

In the middle of the season last year, Mickey was having a good streak. His batting was in full swing, so to speak. He had a streak of hits in 16 straight games, was batting 329, and had 21 homers by the fourth of July. But he wanted more -- he wanted the circuit. Hit for the circuit, and the sports page will include an additional half column with your name at the top. One day he got another chance. The Rome Braves were in Charleston, playing the RiverDogs of the South Atlantic League.

In the first inning Mickey swung at the first pitch he saw, and hit it over the fence. Now that is a comfortable start for a player in any ball game. The next time up he got a single. Perfect so far. His next at-bat came in the fifth inning, two men on base; the count went to three and two. Mickey took his usual smooth swing, not trying to kill the ball but looking for a couple of RBI's. He lofted it to right field, but some twenty yards short of the fence. One more RBI but an easy out. Well, I can't expect a hit every time I come to bat, thought Mickey. The next time however, he hit into the same corner and made it to second base standing up.

When he came to bat for the fifth time, in the top of the ninth inning, his team was winning 8 to 1, so there was really no pressure for Mickey even to get on base. But every ball player is interested in his own record, his own averages, as well as the good of the team and the team averages. You can always use another hit. And this time Mickey couldn't help thinking that all he needed was a triple to join the elite group of players who had hit for the circuit. His promise to the memory of Yogi Berra. "That fly ball I hit into the right field corner in the fifth inning,"

11

thought Mickey, "would have been a triple if only it had been ten feet higher. I can do it; I know I can."

With that, and his eye on the right field corner, he waited for the pitch he wanted. Batting left-handed, he liked it a little low and a little on the inside. He let two strikes go by, one high down the middle, one high on the outside corner. Oh and two the count. Then came what he was looking for: a fast ball low and in, just what he wanted. He drilled it into the right field corner and could see that the fielder would never catch it. It would be a sure three-bagger off the fence, bouncing around in the corner.

He headed off for first base at top speed; didn't want to tarry and risk getting thrown out at third. As he was rounding first and heading for second, he heard a roar go up from the crowd. His fly ball had hit the fence all right, but it hit the top of the fence and bounced out into the street. It was a home run. Mickey slowed down to a trot, adding numbers in his mind. That makes 23 homers. "Shucks," he thought, "I could hit my 23rd homer anytime. Too bad. It's rare that one ever gets a chance to hit for the circuit. Darn."

He kept thinking as he came around second base. His team didn't need this run -- not when the score was 8 to 1 in the ninth. But he needed the circuit.

So he stopped at third base and stood there on the bag, put his hands in his pockets, and looked around as though daring anyone to question him. Another roar went up, even greater than the one that had accompanied the home-run ball bouncing over the fence, as the crowd realized what he was trying to do.

12

Mickey was going to stay where he was. In his book, he had hit for the circuit. Although he wasn't exactly sure what was going to happen next, he knew it would be interesting. It would be interesting to see how the score-keepers handled this and what the sports commentators would have to say in the morning papers. But in any case he knew Yogi would be proud of him. He knew he had hit for the circuit and he was sure Yogi knew it too.

THE END

Wrong Answer

"Holy Cow! Would you look at this!"

"What have you got, Pete?"

"Her name is Anita Hancock. She's a soccer star with a record like you won't believe."

"Don't say 'like' to mean 'such as'."

"All right, Doctor Fowler. 'A record such as you won't believe'."

"Well then, let's get her. Women's soccer is one thing that needs a boost."

"It might not be that easy. In fact, there may be a problem."

Pete Longwood and Nick Constantine worked in the Admissions Office of Stanford University. Every year Stanford receives over 20,000 applications for the 1,200 or so slots in the freshman class. That means a ratio of only six percent acceptances, one of the lowest in the nation, equaled by only a couple of snooty Ivy League colleges. Pete and Nick's job was to sort through these thousands of applications for entry and classify their recommendations as "definitely in," "probable," "possible," "unlikely," and

15

"no way." They also had a separate pile classified by athletic ability or other outstanding extracurricular attributes. Furthermore, the "definitely in" and "probable" piles involved difficult additional work in making recommendations for the granting of the limited athletic and academic scholarships available. Their work was difficult and painstaking, but they both appreciated its significance and enjoyed the sense of importance it gave them.

There were other considerations as well. Stanford likes students who are leaders, who had been presidents of their high-school class or captains of their sports team, or had shown talent and ability in other extra-curricular activities such as the debating society, the school band or chorale, art and drama activities, the chess team, computer club, WWF, ASPCA, NRA, NAACP, AARP, FLAG, ABC, and PDQ. Stanford loves diversity. Stanford is not satisfied merely to give the appearance of tolerance for variations among human beings. Stanford likes real differences -- even real oddballs perhaps, but with outstanding athletic talents and outstanding IQ's and other outstanding features. Stanford is not like Harvard and Yale and Princeton, who want the same kind of students that graduated a hundred or two hundred years ago and are not likely to threaten the *status quo* with a lot of new ideas.

Sometimes candidates with top qualifications in one aspect lose out because of low rankings elsewhere. It was a tough job, and although Longwood and Constantine did not have the final say in these cases, their recommendations went a long way toward the ultimate decision regarding any particular candidate.

"Problem? What problem?" said Nick. "We need some outstanding women soccer players. Women's sports, and especially soccer, are fields we are trying to beef up, you know."

"Yes, I know... but her SAT's... I have never seen anything like this. Everything looks good until you come to her SAT's, and then... Holy Cow! I think we'd better call Wittgenstein and get his take on this."

"Who?"

"Doctor Witt. You know, the head of the Psychology Department. He is also supposed to be an admissions consultant, although he hardly ever shows up. This time I think we need him. There is definitely something weird going on here."

* * * * *

Anita Hancock grew up in Murfreesboro, Tennessee, where her father was on the faculty of the local high school and her mother taught at the community college. Neither of her parents had gone to Yale or Princeton or any fancy schools like that, but had their degrees from the local college and the state university. They were good teachers and were well liked and successful, but did not have what one might call spectacular careers in their academic fields. However, their only daughter, Anita, was an outstanding student from kindergarten on. She was admitted to Mensa when she was twelve years old, and she won most of the prizes and awards that were ever offered in any of the

17

schools she attended. Her parents enjoyed Anita's success vicariously, hoping she might fulfill some of their own frustrated aspirations.

Anita took her academic kudos in stride, paying little attention to her grades, which seemed to stay on top by their own accord. Her real thrill and challenge she found on the athletic field, namely the soccer field, or "Association Football" field, AF, as some old timers still occasionally called it.

She didn't really like her reputation as one of the smartest girls ever to attend Jefferson Davis High School, and it seems that she intentionally let some of her grades slip from A+ to A, and then to A- and even some to B+. She was well aware of the fact that boys didn't like girls who were too smart.

In grade school she had played soccer with the boys, and was just as fast as they were, and even faster and better than some of them. When she got to high school, naturally she did well right from the start, but then her love of soccer suddenly got a tremendous boost her junior year. The reason was a new classmate named Ahmed Akbar, a Syrian exchange student spending his Junior Year Abroad in the United States.

Akbar, like so many foreigners from places like Brazil, Italy, and Nepal, had grown up in a soccer atmosphere and had skills far beyond anything possessed by most American kids. Early on, he spotted Anita's prominent talents, including her athletic talents, and she was most delighted to have him take an interest in her. In short, they hit it off,

18

primarily in the field of their common interest, the soccer field. However, their mutual interest soon spread further afield, to other extracurricular fields, as it were. Lots more. In other words, they started seeing each other, and before soccer season was half over, Anita decided she was in love.

It was the first time she had ever been in love, and she wasn't quite sure how to handle it. So she decided to relax and enjoy it. Now, with Ahmed her personal coach, she blossomed on the soccer field as never before. Her junior year was the happiest time of her life. She was the star, and was voted captain of the team for the following year. But her euphoria did not last. When the school year ended, Akbar of course had to go back to Syria. Anita thereupon decided that she would be as miserable as possible all summer, and that she would enjoy none of the activities she had always participated in with her family and friends in previous years, on the beach or at the lake or anyplace else. Then she decided she did not want to go back to school for her senior year; she wanted to go to Syria and marry Akbar and play with him there -- play soccer there.

"I don't think that would be such a good idea," said her father.

"Has he asked you to marry him?" said her mother, certainly not supporting the idea, but curious nevertheless.

"No, but I am sure he would if I gave him some encouragement."

"Well then, don't encourage him," said her mother. "You are far too young to consider marriage. You must finish high school and get a college degree, and then look around and catch your breath and see where you are before you decide what you want to do with your life."

"I already know what I want to do. I'm going to play soccer. In Syria every town has a soccer team. Sometimes two or three."

"Well, you are underage. All this talk is ridiculous."

"I'll be 18 next year and after that I can do anything I want to."

"Well, you are not 18 now, and you are going back to Jefferson Davis High School and get your degree before you do anything else."

Apparently Akbar felt much the same way about Anita that she felt about him. He wrote to her frequently throughout that summer and the early weeks of the fall semester, urging her to keep developing her talents on the soccer field. He even said he would like to see her again sometime. He never exactly said anything about marriage, but he always sent her his love. Mostly he urged her to keep in shape and go on with her soccer, and to remember some of the pointers he had given her.

So Anita did it. She put her energies and talents into the soccer field and won many more awards that year. She was her school's all-time high scorer, was named to the All-

State Women's Soccer squad, and won the John C. Calhoun Award for the most valuable player in her league.

Her parents made Anita take the SAT exams that September; they were determined that Anita would go on to a college, and a good one. Rice or Emory or Stanford were the places her father particularly had in mind, places where he might have liked to go to college himself, but never had the opportunity. Anita's response: "I want to go to Syria and play soccer. I don't want to go to college; I have told you that. I'll be eighteen by then anyway, and you won't be able to make me go."

"We'll see about that," said her parents. "Now you be a good girl and go and take the SAT like every other sensible kid is doing."

"And don't call me a kid."

"Well, don't act like one."

"All right, all right, I'll take the stupid SAT. Are you satisfied? But don't count on anything."

"That's fine. Now, let's finish supper."

* * * * *

So Pete and Nick debated whether to see Dr. Wittgenstein for his opinion on Anita Hancock's case.

21

"This is a waste of time," said Nick. "She should go into the reject pile with no more questions asked. A monkey answering at random could have gotten a better SAT score."

"Do you mean a smart monkey, or just any monkey?"

"Oh, come on. You know what I mean."

"Yeah, well I mean there is something weird going on here, and I would like to find out what it is. Nobody could be this dumb. Even a monkey or a soccer player."

"What do expect from Wittgenstein?" said Nick.

"Well, in the first place, he is good on statistics -- on bell curves and probabilities and that sort of thing. You can sometimes analyze a specific case against the bell curve and determine with a high degree of confidence whether there has been tampering or other unusual influence involved. There is typically a possible range for outliers to any bell curve, and tampering may create tell-tale outliers completely beyond the acceptable range."

"I think this case is a no-brainer. She couldn't get into a dog-training school with a score like this. We should just reject her."

"Maybe that's what we will do. Probably is. We reject the vast majority of cases anyway, and can certainly reject one more. I don't think we have ever been criticized for rejecting too many, have we?"

"Pete Sampras was in the 'unlikely' pile at first."

"Pete Sampras was something special. And I think this Anita Hancock may be something special too. I really would like to hear what Wittgenstein has to say."

"All right, we'll do it."

So they decided to have a consultation with Wittgenstein. After all, he was supposed to be available as a consultant to the Admissions Office. Besides, Nick wanted to see what Dr. Wittgenstein looked like. He wasn't sure he had ever met him.

*   *   *   *   *

In due course, Anita received an important-looking envelope from the Stanford Admissions Office. Quite sure of what it would say, she waited until suppertime to open it, in the presence of her parents, where she could show them her rejection. She had taken care to see that her application, with the failing SAT scores she had carefully contrived, would be rejected without question.

She was surprised and astonished, and dismayed as well -- although her parents were quite delighted -- when she opened it and found not a rejection but a letter of acceptance. How could this be? She had made sure. Now, hard as it was to believe, Stanford had accepted her application. The letter went on to say that Anita Hancock would receive (not "was being offered," but "would receive" -- Stanford was definite on this) -- "would receive a full scholarship based upon your athletic and academic qualifications, etc. etc."

23

There was a note at the bottom of the letter, handwritten by the Director of Admissions himself: "The Leland Stanford Junior University is delighted that you will be joining our family next fall. Both your athletic record and your academic record based on your SAT's are the most remarkable we have seen in years. We admire your outstanding athletic talents and recognize your genius. We congratulate and welcome you."

Anita couldn't believe it. "They have made some mistake," she blurted out. "I know my SAT's were terrible."

Still, she did not go so far as to tell her parents that she had intentionally answered the SAT questions incorrectly so she wouldn't have to go to college.

However, old Doctor Wittgenstein, at Stanford, saw through her. "This young lady is a genius," he told Longwood and Constantine. "Get her if you possibly can."

"Genius?" said Nick? "Her SAT score is the worst I have ever seen. She got a zero."

"That is exactly what I mean," said Wittgenstein. "She is a 999 at least."

"A what?"

"A 999. Top one-tenth of one percent of the population. In other words, one in a thousand."

"You mean, like Mensa?" said Pete?"

"No, much more than that. The Triple Nine Society is twenty times more restrictive than Mensa. Mensa includes anyone who scores in the top two per cent on any one of a number of tests one can choose from. A lot of Mensa people couldn't have gotten into Stanford, or even Yale, and besides, many of them are overweight nonathletic types."

"I think this one must be in the *bottom* two percent," interjected Nick.

"No," said Wittgenstein, "to be in the bottom two percent you would have to get a few questions right. Even monkeys could do that."

"So?"

"So, the only way you could get all the questions *wrong* is to know what all the *right* answers are. She is a genius."

THE END

Connecting

You might not think this story very funny unless you have studied a little German or maybe one or two other languages.

One of the big problems that foreigners have in learning German is the highly inflected grammar, particularly the endings of nouns and their modifiers. For example, a simple word like the definite article, "the," in English, has as many as six different forms in German, depending on which of three genders the noun may possess, and which of four different cases the noun may fall into, all of which possibilities are doubled with consideration of singular and plural. Some people love complications. They are the ones who should study German.

For instance, there are certain prepositions that always call for their following nouns to be in the dative case, with appropriate dative case endings. Then there are some prepositions that always call for the accusative case (also called the objective case). A few even call for the genitive (or possessive) case. And then there are those prepositions that can take either the dative or the accusative case, letting the action of the verb decide, perhaps according to whether or not motion is involved.

So it behooves the student early on to memorize the list of prepositions that take the dative case, and the list of prepositions taking the accusative case. I clearly remember, from my own first meager studies in that language, memorizing "*aus, bei, gegenüber, mit, nach, zeit, von, zu,*" the "dative" group.

* * * * *

I was spending a few weeks last year on an isolated Caribbean island off the coast of Central America, enjoying the solitude while working on a book of short stories I was putting together. One day I met a Swedish woman, a tourist apparently, who wasn't bad looking and even seemed interesting enough to engage in conversation. Unlike that of many Scandinavians and other northern Europeans, her English was only fair, even halting, I thought. Then she spotted the German book I had with me, for I had been trying to refresh my own halting German at the time. (I wanted to speak in their own language to the few peripatetic German hikers and wanderers who had discovered that remote corner of the world.) Seeing her glancing at my German book, I asked her, "*Sprechen Sie zufällig Deutsch?*"

"*Nur ein bischen*" -- just a little -- she replied, slowly and gently. "*Ich habe etwas studiert...*" Then, showing that she had indeed studied a bit, she continued, in her lovely, lilting Swedish accent: "*Aus, bei, gegenüber, mit, nach, zeit, von, zu.*"

I laughed out loud, and replied, "*Bis, durch, für, gegen, ohne, um,*" the "accusative" group.

Still laughing, we settled for having a -- mostly silent -- cup of tea together. Fortunately we both knew what *eine Tasse Tee* meant. Two different cultures connecting in one language that belonged to neither of them.

I never saw her again, but I hope she is still laughing too.

THE END

The Prediction

He suddenly got an idea. An inspiration. A way out of his quandary. It would hurt her, it is true, but it would hurt less than the alternative. Bobby Aschenhill was a soldier, serving "over there" at the time of this story, but he was a compassionate fellow -- he didn't want to hurt anyone -- not any more than was necessary.

* * * * *

Bobby had grown up in Reading, Pennsylvania, a place that called itself a "Typical American Town." He was the youngest of three brothers in a typical American family, if, in fact, there is any such thing. Maybe the typical town does not exist either, for certainly every town is different in its own way, but Reading, and Bobby's family, were both pretty ordinary.

Reading was a coal town. At least it had been that in the nineteenth century, for it was in the area of the first big anthracite coal deposits found in this country. People, including Bobby's ancestors, soon made a lot of money in the coal industry, and also in its associate, the railroad industry. Bobby's great-great-grandfather -- or perhaps it was three or four greats -- had made his pile in coal, so to speak, and by the time he was in his middle fifties he went on to become President of the Reading Railroad. (I first

31

learned about the Reading Railroad from playing Monopoly as a kid -- "Take a Ride on the Reading" -- but was curious enough to look it up in the encyclopedia and found that it was really real.)

Anyway, even though the Aschenhill family fortunes had been rolling downhill somewhat since the heydays of the railroads and coal-fired steam engines, there was still enough money remaining in the family coffers for the Aschenhills to consider themselves Upper Middle Class, or possibly even Lower Upper Class. One way Bobby's father helped to maintain the family social status was to send his boys to the best New England preparatory schools he could get them into -- Milton, Andover, Hotchkiss -- places like that. The status of such schools in New England seemed socially superior to that of schools in Pennsylvania, filled as they were with so many offspring of coal miners and railroad workers. So Bobby got Hotchkiss.

Bobby liked Hotchkiss all right, studied as much as was necessary, and learned to ski and play hockey, which was both socially acceptable and more fun than schoolwork. However, by the time of his spring semester as a sophomore, Bobby began to look around the town for even more extracurricular activities, namely girls. The local girls liked the Hotchkiss boys, most of whom were clean-cut Americans, reasonably well dressed, and with relatively few police records or contagious diseases. Besides, as the girls soon learned, the boys generally had some money, and some of them, seniors anyway, even had a car, and they would let you ride around with them and go places and do things.

Robin Flanagan was one of the "townies." Her father, Rob Flanagan, had been a guide who arranged hunting parties during the season, but now ran a canoe rental operation on the Housatonic River for vacationers from New York or families of the Hotchkiss boys. That is where Robin met Bobby. Bobby and one or two of his friends, one fine day in spring, were out for an adventure on the river. Robin was impressed with Bobby from the start. She liked his name, Robert, the same name as her father's, a good omen. She liked his reasonably good looks, his skill with a canoe paddle, and his gentlemanly willingness to pay without question her father's exorbitant boat-rental charges.

It was easy for her to think that she could fall in love with him. So that's what she did.

The timing was good. Bobby had learned to handle his schoolwork and sports activities competently, and he was now beginning to spend a little more time thinking of the opposite sex, especially girls. He was a little shy by nature, and Robin's fresh and uninhibited style made it easy for him to development a relationship with her. Not a relationship in the modern sense of a boy and a girl actually having *relations* with each other, but the relationship of two friends who enjoyed each other's company and the diversion it offered from their respective daily routines. At first, anyway.

So they started seeing each other on a regular basis, which, by the fall term of Bobby's senior year, had indeed developed into the more intimate type of relationship we were intimating a moment ago. In short, they decided they were in love and had to show each other, when opportunities presented themselves, how deep their love reached, so to speak.

In March of Bobby's senior year, the United States managed to get itself involved in one more of the many wars we like to get into, whether started by ourselves or by others. Although there was not yet a national draft, or military conscription, at that time, you never knew when it might come along. Bobby and some of his classmates, even before graduation, were already talking about joining up and getting some military service behind them. Besides, if you joined up instead of waiting to be drafted, you sometimes had a choice and got better assignments, and furthermore it looked good on your 201 record. They were a patriotic bunch, loved flag-waving, brass bands, and parades -- and of course the thought of slaying the enemy, particularly if he were a Saracen, a heathen, or just an ordinary terrorist. There are a number of patriotic little towns scattered across New England with names like "Freedom" and "Liberty." Look on any map.

Bobby told Robin, who by then was his acknowledged sweetheart, that he wanted to join up, and asked her if she would marry him. She jumped with joy, naturally, and wanted to get married immediately, while the iron was hot, maybe even on his Graduation Day. Bobby bought her a nice square-cut 1.5 carat diamond engagement ring. However, knowing that his parents wouldn't feel too happy about all this -- about his attachment to some unknown little totty who probably had never even been presented to society -- he persuaded her that they should hold off on the actual wedding for a while longer.

When Bobby's parents did learn of his plans, they were doubly aghast, first that he was thinking of getting married at all, and second that he was thinking of going into the Army. He wouldn't even be twenty until that August. But dear Robin was the main thing on Bobby's mind. She was the one he loved and cared for, and the one that loved and cared for him.

"Oh, my love!" she proclaimed as passionately as any Juliet at the Globe Theatre, "Please don't go... But, if you do think you have to go, I will be here for you always, whether we are married or not. You are the only one I could ever love." She didn't want to lose this fellow.

After a few days back in Reading with his parents and some of his old high school friends, followed by a couple of weeks with his dear Robin in Connecticut, Bobby did join the Army and was promptly sent to Fort Benning -- wherever that is -- for his basic training. Ten weeks later he was a soldier. He thereupon had a brief period of additional training as an infantryman, or rifleman, as some of them preferred to be called, at Fort Bragg. In spite of Army recommendations against it, Robin came to Fayetteville, where she took an apartment for four weeks to be with her dear fiancé as much as possible until his imminent deployment overseas. Bobby was delighted to have her there where he could see her, at least on weekends, and enjoyed the distraction she provided from his exercises and training in desert warfare.

In due course the day came for him to depart, and accordingly he left, with his unit, bound for an obscure country in the Middle East. It used to be called the Near East, but now in these modern times it was the Middle East; I suppose because it is in the middle of most of the hottest action these days.

* * * * *

Bobby didn't see any fighting, though. Not at first. The initial responsibilities for his unit involved inspections, formations, exercises, and physical training, or "PT," to keep in shape and alert. He promptly began to spend his off-duty hours getting acquainted with the little community near his base. He was interested to learn that it had once been part of a French colony in the old days, and there were still people there who spoke French, including a few locals and even some entire French families. Bobby had studied some French during his years at Hotchkiss, and now had an opportunity to try it out in a real-life situation. As long as things were quiet, the troops were allowed to visit the little towns in the area on their off-duty hours.

Bobby had always admired oriental carpets, or "Persian rugs," as they used to be called, whether or not they came from Persia. His family's home had many lovely carpets and tapestries, some quite valuable, and he found carpets, with their history and origins, fascinating.

So that is why one afternoon he was delighted to discover the *"Grand Magazin de Tapisserie"* in the heart of the old town. He went in, and from that moment his life was never the same again. He found, therein, not only a plethora of lovely carpets, but also the lovely nubile daughter of the French owner of the establishment. Now it had been several weeks since Bobby had seen his dear sweet Robin, and her image had begun to fade somewhat in his mind under the pressing distractions of his military training and deployment. It wasn't something that Bobby planned or even wanted. Absence, and time, will do that; sometimes you can't help it.

As you have now guessed, Bobby fell in love again, this time at first sight. For the next several weeks thereafter, Bobby spent every possible free off-duty moment visiting with Michèle, or just lingering in and about the shop if she were busy.

Bobby was also wise enough to carefully curry favor with Michèle's father and mother, especially her mother. Michèle enjoyed his attentions, bolstered as they were by frequent gifts he would bring to the family from the Army commissary or post exchange -- sugar, butter, eggs, and other foodstuffs, not to mention scented soap and perfume for the ladies and a bottle or two of forbidden Scotch whisky and some cigars for *Monsieur le Tapissier*. After a few weeks of this routine, which stretched on to a couple of months, Bobby decided that he really was in love this time and that his engagement to Robin, eleven months earlier, had been a mistake, an error stemming from misdirected youthful exuberance. The sad truth is that, with notable exceptions, teen-age love, though it may be hot, may also be short lived.

Michèle was the one he wanted to be his wife, the one he wanted to spend the rest of his life with, after he was able to get out of this stupid Army that never seemed to do anything.

Of course, he never told Michèle that he was already engaged to a woman back home. That was his own problem, and something he would have to work out later. He never lied about it; just never mentioned it. Keeping silent isn't quite the same as lying, he told himself. He did tell Michèle of his love for *her*, however, and was delighted to hear her respond in kind. *M. le Tapissier* and his wife were beginning to suspect the truth about what was going on between these children, but thought the possibility of having their daughter marry an American was all right. Even a good idea. It might open up business connections and commercial opportunities in the United States after this little domestic war got put out with the help of the Americans.

Until now Bobby and his unit had seen no combat action since his arrival in country. For Bobby there had been nothing more exciting than physical training exercises broken by occasional security guard duty and convoy coverage, "riding shotgun," as the troops called it, in an armored personnel carrier at the head, or sometimes at the rear, of a supply convoy running form the port of entry to the interior.

Now all that was about to change. The militants' influence was expanding and encroaching on an area that had previously been cleared -- an area Bobby's unit was responsible for. There had been several assassinations, and two or three villages had recently fallen to the enemy. Bobby's battalion was now given the job of regaining these villages and clearing out the enemy. Bobby served as a good soldier and did what he was told. It took a month to clear and hold the first of these three villages, which was only about fifty kilometers from the Army base, but for that entire month Bobby had to go without seeing Michèle at all. However, being away from her that long made him realize how much he really did love her, and thereupon at the first opportunity after he got back to the base he told her he wanted to marry her. She talked it over with her parents, and they all promptly agreed in principle that it would be all right, even that it was a good idea, but wisely acknowledged that this was not quite the time for a · wedding. It would be better to wait a little while.

That fitted in neatly with Bobby's confused plans and hopes, for he was still committed to Robin back home and would have to do something about that. By now he well realized that he had been hasty in getting engaged to her. After all, he asked himself, was it fair to expect her to stay at home like an old maid and not enjoy the companionship of other people she had known? Should she limit her social activities and exclude any young men about town? He began to feel remorse at having imposed such a severe limitation on the range of life's activities available to sweet Robin. He still cared for her -- he really did, but as a distant friend now -- and he asked himself whether he had made her happier by becoming engaged to her, or not. Often his answer was not. He concluded that it would make her life happier if he gave her her freedom.

She had written to him regularly, telling him how much she loved him and how much she missed him, and how she was staying true to him in his absence and how she would wait as long as it took for him to get back so they could be married and live happily ever after and have lots of children. That's what she said. It was almost as though she had gotten her words out of a novel by Barbara Cartland or Danielle Steele.

Now as I have pointed out, Bobby was a compassionate fellow, even if he didn't have all his ducks in a row. He didn't want to hurt Robin -- no more than necessary anyway -- but he knew now that Robin and he were not suited for each other. The sight of Michèle taught him that it had been a mistake to get engaged and tie Robin down like that. He wanted to make the break-up, and his traitorous behaviour, as easy on Robin as possible.

Then he had an idea. Clearing "Village Number One" last month had not been easy. There had been casualties, both military and civilian -- casualties among the enemy and casualties among the Americans. Most of our casualties came from exploding mortar fragments and improvised explosive devices set as booby traps in doors and entryways of buildings we had to clear of the enemy. Corporal Thomas Rainey, one of Bobby's best Army buddies, was one of those killed at "Village Number One," just last week, with a fragment through the head. And now plans were being made to clear "Village Number Two."

What gave Bobby his idea was his regret and sorrow at the thought of how Robin would be hurt by the news that he was dropping her for another woman. "There is nothing more painful to a girl" -- Bobby had once read somewhere -- "than the realization that another woman has taken her place in the heart of her loved one." Bobby was a compassionate fellow. He couldn't do that to her. It would hurt her less if he just left this world, even if he had to die to do it. That way he would at least leave her with some sympathy and maybe even a few pleasant old memories.

He decided he would get his Platoon Sergeant to write a letter to her, telling her he had been killed in action. Bobby would dictate the letter, but it had to be in the Sergeant's handwriting. Yes, that's what he would do.

But his wise sergeant would have nothing to do with it. He was appalled that Bobby would suggest such a thing.

Bobby, however, was undaunted; it only meant he had to take the task upon himself. He would write the letter, disguising his handwriting, pretending that he was the sergeant. He would write it with his left hand. He tried practicing, and found that if he wrote very slowly, with his hand sort of upside down, he could make legible letters that looked as though they came from an honest soldier writing under difficult conditions.

So that's what he did. He wrote the letter, saying that Corporal Aschenhill had been a good soldier, done his duty, and had been bravely facing the dangerous task of the final clearing of "Village Two" when he was struck and killed by a piece of shrapnel to the head. Bobby wanted to make it as easy on Robin as possible, so in the letter he went on to say that his death had been almost immediate and that he hadn't suffered much. The letter ended by saying that

41

"Bobby often spoke of you and of how he could never love anybody else in this world." A forged signature read, "Sergeant Emilio Bustamente," a fictitious name of course. Wouldn't want to make trouble for anyone.

"There," thought Bobby, "that should do it, without hurting her too much." He shot it off through the APO; it took four days to get to the United States.

Three weeks later Mr. and Mrs. Aschenhill, Bobby's parents, received a registered letter from the Office of the Adjutant General, Department of the Army. "Oh my God," cried Mrs. Aschenhill, "I just knew something terrible was going to happen to him."

Mr. Aschenhill opened the letter. "We regret to inform you... "

He had to sit down. "... Corporal Achenhill was killed in action on November 11 ..."

"... bravely leading his squad in a clearing operation ..."

Painfully he read on: "... died instantly from a sniper bullet to the head... "

They called their other two sons, Bobby's brothers, to give them the sad news. Then Mrs. Aschenhill, between her sobs and tears, said, "I suppose we should tell that Flanagan girl too."

"I'll call her," said her husband. And he did.

* * * * *

"Hello, is that you, Robin?"

"Yes, this is Robin. Oh, Mr. Aschenhill, I was so sorry to hear about Bobby. I thought of calling you, but I didn't want to add to your pain."

"We just learned today. When did you find out?"

"Why, I got a letter from Bobby's platoon commander a couple of weeks ago, around the end of October. I was sure you would have known. He described Bobby's heroism in the process of final clearing of some place they called 'Village Number Two.' Bobby was hit in the head by a piece of shrapnel and died almost immediately, without suffering very much. That's what the letter said."

(What Robin didn't tell Mr. and Mrs. Aschenhill was that upon receiving the false letter about Bobby's supposed death she promptly called a fellow named Sean McIverson, a chap that neither Bobby nor the Aschenhills had ever heard of. McIverson was not in at the moment, so she left a message on his voice mail. It was simply, "Sean, this is Robin. Just calling to say we can set our wedding date any time now.")

"That's strange," thought Mr. Aschenhill out loud. "Our official letter says he died on November 11 and that he was killed by a sniper bullet while his unit was clearing that 'Village Number Two,' but all the other details are the same as your letter described them."

THE END

43

Rainy Day

My husband is a nice guy. He really is. And I love him a lot -- I really do. He's my second husband, of course. My first husband was a mistake. His name was Mervin, but he let me call him Mernie, and he wasn't even Jewish. Captious cad, nothing ever pleased him. Why I married him I'll never know. Yes, I do know. I was sort of pushed into it. My parents had some social aspirations and Mernie's parents were socially prominent in our town. I was a dutiful daughter, darn it, and went along with my parents' plans for me. You can read books about bad marriages, or how smart women make dumb choices, written by people like Dr. Connell Cowan and Melvyn Kinder, but I didn't know about them back then.

I wanted to be a writer ever since I was a freshman in high school, or fresh woman, as some of us more thoughtful girls used to say sometimes, only half in jest. But I never got much encouragement until I was in college and got into a Creative Writing class. I married Mernie soon after graduation, but it didn't last long. Mernie's parents were decent and decorous people, but Mernie wasn't like them at all, and I don't want to talk about him. I'd rather talk about Richard, my second husband, my real husband, the one I love. He had already been married and divorced by the time I met him, so no one can accuse me of breaking up his marriage with my feminine wiles or guiles. However, I might have done so, or at least tried, if I had known him sooner and the opportunity had arisen.

45

Before meeting Richard I had been divorced for over four years, without any man at all in my life. I was rigorously sublimating my inherent romantic urges and concentrating on my writing career, or what I hoped would become a career. I was scrimping along financially as fashion editor on a small town newspaper that had not quite yet gone out of business, while working on the side getting an occasional maudlin piece of bathos into one of the slick women's magazines and even doing a couple of travel articles. My inchoate sex life was still dead, or at least dormant. Then one day my good friend and co-worker Sandra Reischauer said she had an acquaintance she wanted me to meet. She showed me a picture of him with some other people taken at the beach last summer. He was remarkably good looking and appeared to be an active outdoors type of man, who -- she explained -- also liked books and was able to read, in spite of his somewhat raffish air. And he had even been to Paris once, she pointed out. "I am sure you will like him," she insisted.

Now Sandra had a happy marriage of her own, and was a person you could trust. I looked at myself in the mirror; not too bad, I thought. Maybe it was time for me to think of the possibility of developing a relationship or something -- bring something, or someone, into my life -- while I still had something worth looking at. Yes, although I was fairly happy and doing fairly well with my life now, I realized I was missing a man. As I started thinking more about it, I even got myself worked up a little, something that hadn't happened in years. Yes, maybe it's time to set the literary world of the mind aside for a moment and look into the sybaritic world of the physical for a change.

46

"All right, why not," I told Sandra.

"Splendid," said Sandra. "Come to supper Saturday; I'll seat you two together. His name is Dick." Dick -- a good omen, I thought, and I let my imagination run ahead as it had not done for some time.

That's how it all started. Dick and I were immediately attracted to each other and started seeing each other the first chance we got. We promptly discovered that we were compatible. Maybe I filled a hole in his life; he certainly filled one in mine. We were married soon after that, and have been very happy ever since. Or at least I can say reasonably happy.

You see, Richard brought some obligations along with him into our marriage. As I may have mentioned, he too had been married before, but unlike me, he had children to support and was still paying alimony. His wife, Raquel, had gotten custody of the two girls, but Richard, who was a little older than I, was still supporting his son in college. Richard had a good job as regional sales manager for a sporting goods company, and was a conscientious worker, but was not rolling in dough. He worked hard and fulfilled his obligations dutifully. For that I respected him. But I had my own busy life and career to work on, and I never resented Richard's inability to devote as much time to me as I might have liked. Not at first. Not for a long time.

Richard was such a dear, sincere, kind person, that I could not bear to suggest that I needed anything more in marriage. Richard knew I was always gentle and warm and welcoming whenever he came home, even if he had been

47

working late. About six months ago he took on a higher position in his company, with more responsibility and longer hours, but with a significant increase in salary. With his Yankee upbringing he wanted to pay off all his debts from past years and do what was best for his family, including me. I had to admire him for his devotion and self-sacrifice. Nowadays he hardly ever got away for the hunting expeditions that he used to love, or for fishing weekends on a lake in upper New York State that he knew about.

Then one day last month he came home about eight o'clock with a big grin on his face and a long thin package under his arm with something sticking out the end of it. "I brought you a present," he said. What on earth? I opened it up, and there was a sparkling new shiny fishing rod with a chrome-silver reel attached. What in...?

"Honey, how about you and me taking off for the weekend and going up to the lake?"

"Fine," I said. "That's something I have always wanted to do." At least that's what I said. After all, he let me teach him to play cribbage on our honeymoon. Tit for tat is fair, I thought. And besides, I rather liked the idea of going off somewhere for the weekend. Going off anyway, whether or not with fish. Just his saying the words made it sound rather romantic, although if the fishing was good I didn't know how much time would be left over for flirtation or romance -- romance in the sense of the fulfillment of my lascivious ideas on how to bring to life the image of my carnal thoughts, and how best to enliven and manifest some resurgent passion.

"Sounds great," I added, giving him a good kiss just like I always do when he comes home late, whether he needs it or not.

So we did it. We went to the cabin on the lake, a four-hour drive on a good day. Dick was supposed to get off work at noon that Friday so we could get up there in time to taste the sapid evening air and "drop a few hooks in the water" before nightfall. However, as it turned out, something came up, as things so often do, and he didn't get off until four-thirty, in the middle of a summer-afternoon rainstorm. Oh well, we'll have all day Saturday and part of Sunday for fishing, we said. We thought. Let's go. We can get a bite of supper somewhere on the road when the rain lets up.

We got to the cabin Friday night at 10 o'clock after stopping for something at a fast-food drive-in along the way. It was still raining and the wind was howling when we reached the cabin. Tired from the drive and the week's hard work, we went straight to bed and slept soundly.

"Tomorrow will be delightful," whispered Dick, mostly to himself in his hypnagogic state, as he drifted off to dreamland. "Rain is sometimes good for fish."

The next day it was still rainy and windy when I woke up. Dick was still in bed, but beginning to stir. "Darling," I whispered, "the weather is miserable out there. There's no point in getting up... let's stay in bed a little longer," I said, gently cuddling closer against his warm body. He woke up a little but not too much. Just enough. After a while we both went back to sleep. We slept late and stayed in bed even later. I had no desire to get up; I like to read in bed, and fortunately had with me a book of Maupassant stories. I read one aloud to Dick; I hadn't done that for a long time. He liked it.

After a while he finally got up and made some coffee and toast for a late brunch; then he went out in the rain and tried to fish. Useless. He came back to the cabin about three o'clock, soaking wet and with a long face. Obviously no success. "I'm sorry about the fishing," I said softly and sincerely. "Go have a hot shower; it'll be cocktail time soon."

I went back into the bedroom and stretched out with my book. When Dick came in with a towel wrapped around him, I said, "Here's another story I would like to read to you. Come, lie down a minute." He was agreeable. I only got halfway through the story, and the next thing I knew I was relaxed once more and it was six o'clock, time to catch up on our cocktail hour and put something on the stove for supper.

We had some wine with the meal and a small glass of sherry after that. We talked to each other, something we never seemed to have time for at home. We found each other interesting -- unpressured and tranquil as we were. We decided to go to bed early. There was only one bed, in case I hadn't mentioned it, but we made it do.

Sunday morning we spent part of the time talking in bed, something we rarely had time for back home. The weather was still rainy and miserable, and I think Dick was beginning to enjoy the interior of our warm little cabin and the comfort of our being together with no pressing distractions from our jobs or other activities. Besides, we were learning things about each other we had never known before.

Two clock came soon. I made us some egg-salad sandwiches for brunch. Eggs are good for you, recent studies show. I think I already knew that. Still raining, a light drizzle. Still no fishing. We went back into the bedroom.

Before long it was time to start packing up for the drive home.

"Sorry your fishing weekend was spoiled," I said, in my caring, compassionate tone of voice, when we got back to town, although I didn't really mean it.

"Spoiled?" he said, giving me a kiss. "It was the best fishing weekend I have had in years."

THE END

Short Stories Encore

Point of View

My forebears were from Vermont -- Vermont, New Hampshire, and even Massachusetts -- 'way back. I don't know how they stood it. I mean, it gets COLD up there. I spent part of one winter in Burlington, where my grandparents lived, and later a couple of years in Boston in school, and let me tell you, New England gets COLD. My nephew grew up in Burlington, and later worked in Iowa and Kansas, which he said were even colder than Vermont in the winter. I don't know how that could be possible; it must have REALLY been cold out there. I don't know how people can stand those places.

I lived for a number of years in Washington, DC, working for the government, and that was cold enough for me. Too cold. The first thing I did after I retired was to move SOUTH. I found a pleasant little spot on the water near Beaufort, South Carolina, that I could afford. I love swimming, especially in salt water. I could swim in the creek there behind my house for six or seven months of the year, and the winter months were never so cold that you couldn't play tennis or golf occasionally, at least two or three times a week.

But as I got older it seemed that the winters, even in South Carolina, were longer and colder than I liked. They probably were not really getting any colder; I was probably getting older and more feeble and sensitive. Anyway, I decided to get out of the South Carolina winter for a few weeks and find some place where it was nice and warm.

After methodically checking atlases and climate statistics and weather reports, as well as airline connections and fares, I decided on a little island off the Caribbean coast of Nicaragua, and now this is the fourth time I have been here. The climate is delightfully pleasant, just what I wanted and hoped for. The ocean is warm, around 78 degrees. It is mostly sunny, with occasional ten percent cloud cover or a little tropical shower. Air temperature also averages 78 degrees, sometimes getting up into the middle or high eighties in the afternoon and falling to the low seventies at night. Oh, how delightful it is to be warm in January while the poor folks back in the United States and other places are shoveling snow and struggling with freezing temperatures and ice storms.

Yesterday I met a fellow with an interesting accent who had just arrived to stay here at the same little beach-front lodge where I am staying. Being perfect strangers, we naturally began to talk of the weather. We agreed it was ideal here.

I told him I was from South Carolina, and explained where that was. He was from Cordoba, Argentina, northwest of Buenos Aires. Then I thought: Argentina... that's way down there in the Southern Hemisphere, about as far south of the equator as the United States is north of it. Down there their seasons are backwards from ours, of course. I counted up mentally, adding six months in my head. Here it was early January; down there it must be like early July, as we know it. Early July in most of the United States is usually pleasant and warm.

Just after I had told this fellow that I was here in Nicaragua to get out of the cold back home, I went on to say, "But your place in Argentina -- it must be summer. It can't be cold there now."

"That's right," he said. "I came here to get out of the heat."

THE END

The Robbery

"If I'da known dat, I wouldna did it." That's what Flash said. Those were his words.

Flash was a city kid, through and through. If you had shown him a cow, he wouldn't have known which end to feed the hay into. Flash grew up in a poor neighborhood, where his mother was poor, where their home was a poor tenement house, and where his friends all came from poor families. But Flash was smart. You had to be smart to survive in Flash's neighborhood, which was not only a poor neighborhood but also a tough neighborhood.

If you were smart, like Flash, you belonged to the right gang -- the Vesuvius Gang. If you didn't belong to a gang, or if you belonged to the wrong gang, like the Stromboli Gang, you could get pushed around, and life would be miserable. You would be a nobody. To be somebody, you had to belong to the right gang, the Vesuvius Gang.

Unfortunately, gangs have gotten a bad reputation. But the truth is that the guys that belong to Flash's gang, the Vesuvius Gang, are not really bad guys. Not all of them. Like, Flash wasn't really a bad guy either. It's because of where he lived that sometimes he got, like, into bad situations, and then he had to do, like, what he had to do to survive.

57

Flash wasn't his real name. Flash was just his nickname, but it was the only name most of the kids knew for him. His real name was Kanawa Arijama Washington. Most of the other kids also had nicknames, like Spud, or Zippo, or Flash. Flash got his name because one afternoon he had an emergency situation and he had his pants down, taking a crap in the alley, when the restaurant owner came out the back door and saw him and threatened to call the cops and have him arrested for indecent exposure. He impolitely yelled at Flash, raising his voice and hollering that flashing was illegal, and accusing Flash of embarrassing -- yes, embarrassing -- him. So that's how Flash got to be called Flash. Zippo always went around with his zipper half open; he would say with a "Ha ha" that the girls liked it that way, ready when needed. Some kinda hooey like that. I don't know how Spud and Hickory got their names; I'll ask them some day.

The cops were always bothering us and hassling us whenever they could. Whenever they had time on their hands they would take it out on us. And even when they were supposed to be on duty they would still take it out on us. They were always telling us what to do, and what not to do, like where we couldn't play stick ball, and where we could only play basketball, or where we couldn't go more than three of us at a time into some store, or where we were making too much noise after midnight, somewhere they said was too close to the hospital, even though it wasn't really close at all. Things like that. And they were always "questioning" us, about all sorts of things, whether they were things we had done or knew anything about or not.

Okay, so we smoked a little pot like everybody else did, and did some crack occasionally like everybody else did, or made a few bucks with some sales like everybody else did. But judging from the way the cops got on top of us and hassled us you would have thought we were plotting to fly some loaded drones into the Empire State Building and the Chrysler Building, while in fact we never had any plans like that at all. Mostly all we ever did was just try to do as best we could to protect our turf and take care of ourselves and our brothers, but it was a tough life. We never wanted to hurt nobody for no reason, least ways less they was from the Stromboli bunch of thugs.

*   *   *   *   *

So you can understand why in court one day last October Flash told the judge, "I wouldna did it if I'da known THAT."

All he had done was to politely ask a woman to give him some money so he could buy a sandwich and some new shoes, and she started giving him a hard time. So it was necessary for him to bring out his "persuader," a seven -inch Italian switch-blade knife, razor sharp, just to show her he meant business. But she still didn't get the picture. Didn't realize he was serious, I mean. She tried to snatch her purse back from him, although he was only taking what he needed, but she accidentally cut her arm and shoulder on his knife that he was just holding there as a warning to her. She began yelling and making a scene, which Flash found annoying, so he ran off down the street because he hates scenes. However, though it's hard to believe, some friendly onlookers stopped Flash, and after a bit of a tussle they held him down until the police came.

* * * * *

Haven't I seen you before?" said the judge.

"I dunno. Lotsa people seen me before. I can't remember all of 'em."

"Have you ever been arrested before?"

"Yeah, I guess."

"Young man, when you are speaking to the court, you say, 'Your Honor,' understand?"

"All ri, chur on-uh."

"How many times have you been arrested?"

"A coupla times; I'm not sure zackly."

"Where were you on February 10, 2013?"

"Rye cheer in New York, yer on-uh. I neva goes nowheres. Ise allers rye cheer."

"Were you on Tenth Avenue between 47th and 48th street on February 10, 2013, around 8:30 pm?

"I dunno; I coulda been."

"You were arrested there for breaking and entering a convenience store. Do you remember that?"

"I din' do nuttin'. I jes happen to be at the wrong place at the wrong time."

"You were also arrested on April 23, 2013 for car theft. What do you remember about that?"

"I neva stole no car. Least ways, I din' steal dat one. Zippo de one whut stole it. But Zippo din' have no driver's license, so I hep him a little by driving it a ways for him."

"You have a driver's license? It says here in the police report you were arrested for car theft and for driving without a license."

"No, I ain' got no license neither. I never had one 'cause I never had no car. I never seed no use fo a car in New York. I ain' got no place I could keep a car no how. But I knows how to drive, so I hep Zippo out a little by drivin' his car for him."

"You mean, the stolen car."

"I guess. Yeah, it coulda been stolen, but Zippo wasn't gonna keep it. He was jes' borrin' it for a while. He only needed it for some spare parts."

"Spare parts?"

"Yeah, he needed spare parts for a old car his dead uncle give him, that was the same make and model, and that he was gonna learn to drive so he could get his driver's license, but it wouldn't run so he hadda get it fixed. But it needed some spare parts. I din' steal nothin'. Honest. I was jes' hepping a friend out that needed a little hep."

"All right, tell me what happened on May 27. It says here that you and two others were arrested for breaking into the Modern Jewelery store on 129th Street."

"That ain' ri, chur on-uh. We din' do no break-in. The door was lef unlock, because the man what runs the sto' fergot to lock it."

"And you went in with the purpose of theft and larceny and were accosted by a security guard."

"I din' know they was fixing to steal anything, yer on-uh. I thought they jes' wanted to look around. And we *din't* stole nuttin' neither. All we was doin' was jes' looking around and then this guy with a big gun and a big Security Badge come up and accused us of robbery."

"Your flagitious criminal record doesn't bode very good for you, young man. And now you've been arrested for theft and aggravated assault with a deadly weapon. It is alleged that just last month, on September 16, 2013, you accosted a pregnant woman on Huston Street, severely lacerated her arm and shoulder with a sharp instrument, stole money from her purse, knocked her down, and fled from the scene. What do you have to say for yourself about that?"

"Pregnant, chur on-uh? I din' know she was pregnant. If I'da known she was pregnant, I neva woulda did it."

THE END

Short Stories Encore

The Beauty of This World

Some people will tell you that a great composer, or a great poet, or a great artist, has to suffer, or at least should suffer, as he climbs the parlous path to greatness and fame. I wouldn't know. But I do believe that we don't always appreciate what we have until we lose it. Or maybe until we die. But then...

Beauty and fresh air and peacefulness certainly are things we don't appreciate until we don't have them.

For example, I didn't sufficiently appreciate my wife until after she died. Then I appreciated her. Also, by then we had no more disagreements. And my childhood -- I have enjoyed my childhood more looking back on it than I ever did going through it. And music. I always knew I loved music, but I didn't realize how much I loved music until I started to go deaf in my seventies. Now I can only hear the tubas and the double basses and the drums in the great symphonies. I have tried to follow the score of Beethoven's Ninth, written when Beethoven had already lost his own hearing, but reading notes is not the same as hearing them. It is nowhere nearly so much fun.

But one great thing about great artists, whether they have suffered or not, is that they are supposed to be able to see things that ordinary people are not able to see. Like poets, and maybe composers as well, artists interpret the world for us less well-endowed, less perspicacious, ordinary human beings.

65

How many times have you looked at a haystack in the late afternoon twilight and seen the colors that Claude Monet saw? Or seen the beauty that he saw in a stagnant pool of water sprouting a mass of lilies behind your house or alongside the golf course in that gated community not far from your home?

Beauty and fresh air and peacefulness are things we don't appreciate -- until we don't have them.

* * * * *

In 1748 a young man was born in Paris who, from the time he first wanted anything, wanted to be a painter. His name was Jacques Louis David. Maybe you have heard of him, or seen some of his famous paintings of Napoleon and other notables. Of course, being born in Paris was a good start for a fellow with an ambition to be a French painter. Michelangelo, the sculptor, was lucky to have been born in the shadow of a mountain in Tuscany made of marble. Mozart got a good start merely by being born at the right time and place for his music -- Salzburg in the eighteenth century. Paris was a good place to be born in, in 1748, if you wanted to be an eighteenth century French painter.

When Jacques was growing up, his father sent him to the best schools. The lad was fascinated by things of beauty, like poetry, music, and art -- but especially art -- including the paintings of the old masters. He didn't care much for Latin and mathematics, except for an interest in geometry -- for the proportions and ratios and angles it dealt with, and for the beauty and balance it showed him. Proving the Pythagorean Theorem was less interesting to him than just looking at the 1.62/1.00/0.62 rectangle, the rectangle with the perfect ratios so beloved by Leonardo Fibonacci and the ancient Greeks, for its ideal proportion and balance, a thing of beauty in four straight lines. (If you were to cut a square from a perfect rectangle, the remainder would be another, smaller, perfect rectangle.)

To young Jacques, art was the path to deeper insights and greater understanding of life and love and beauty and nature -- indeed, the world. The finest artists, by means of their beautiful oil paintings, were able to go deeply inside worldly objects and worldly people. They could elicit and reveal to the onlooker the essence of fascinating subjects that were unfathomable to the eyesight of ordinary human beings.

Jacques might have felt these things, but he did not really think about them while studying art. Art to him was a captivating mistress. He was only really happy when he had a pencil or a brush in his hand, and could yield for a moment to his creativity and the driving force within him to put what he saw on to paper or canvas. No, that is not quite correct. Not only what he saw, but also what he felt, what his involuntary emotional reaction was, his reflexive response, his brain activity as stimulated by his vision. Although he would not have said it, and maybe did not even know it, what he was doing was interpreting what he saw and preserving it and its existence and meaning.

His art studies in school had given him a solid knowledge of the techniques of preparing canvasses, grinding colors, mixing paints, turpentine thinners, fixatives, varnish glosses -- all the mechanics of painting. But the inspiration for the creation of something beautiful did not come from studies in school -- it came from within.

Like all fine artists, Jacques was a master at drawing with pen or pencil, although his love was of course painting. His interests and studies took him to Italy as a young man, where he made numerous pencil sketches of his surroundings -- street scenes, landscapes, and people, but he soon realized that his forte was painting people, namely portraits. He was fascinated by the realization that an artist could paint not just what he saw in a subject's face but what he saw in his heart and soul. He was fascinated by the power that resided in an artist's hand -- the ability to reveal the truth, so often hidden from ordinary people whether through ignorance or by design. He gained great expertise in Italy, and was an experienced portrait painter by the time he had to return to his native country.

Back in the land of his birth, his portraits were an immediate success. He was in high demand and painted portraits of many famous political and military leaders, with little regard for their politics or party orientation. Unfortunately, there was great confusion in France in those days.

Especially confusing in Paris were matters of government and politics. Political allegiances were intense and ephemeral. Opposition groups quarreled among themselves. Yesterday's leaders were in prison today. Notables and non-notables, thinkers and non-thinkers, were losing their heads right and left, both figuratively and literally.

Jacques had no deep political convictions -- his devotion was to his art. He was indifferent to politics. However, politics thrust its ugly head into his life willy-nilly, and the subjects of his paintings, whether statesmen, military leaders, or outstanding citizens and philosophers, got him into trouble -- deep trouble. Because his subjects included individuals of all political persuasions, he was accused, from all sides, of being a spy, a traitor, a political enemy.

It wasn't hard in those times to get connected with the wrong groups. Indeed, in Paris in the frantic days of the early 1790's, it was hard not to. It was difficult or impossible to know which were the wrong groups, who the Good Guys were and who the Bad Guys were. They all seemed to be wrong, depending on one's point of view. Today's Good Guys were tomorrow's Bad Guys and today's Bad Guys were yesterday's Good Guys.

Still uninterested in politics, Jacques let the political breezes blow him this way and that, until one fine day in the autumn of 1793 he was arrested, by the forces currently in power, because of his alleged allegiance to groups now out of power. In those hectic days there was no time for civil rights or due process of law or anything like that. David was seized and summarily thrown into prison in the Chateâu Luxembourg -- the Luxembourg Prison.

Now at that time there were lots of evil forces confronting each other, but it so happened that some of the individual prison guards had only meager political convictions. Some of the guards had been conscripted merely because they were available or because of where they happened to be at the time, and not because of their political beliefs or orientation. Some of the kinder ones recognized Jacques for the famous painter that he was, and did what they could to make his time of incarceration a little easier, if not exactly enjoyable.

Life in prison was indeed onerous for the painter, whose heart and soul had floated freely and wildly across many beautiful countrysides and elegant salons. The isolation from the world of people and nature that he loved made his relentless incarceration ever so much more onerous than it would have been for ordinary people. Most prisoners were like a mouse or a rat in a box. An artist, a painter like Jacques, was a bird locked in a cage, unable to fly or even to stretch his wings, barely able to stay alive.

The days and weeks dragged by interminably. Jacques even thought of ending his life although, perhaps fortunately, there were no convenient means of doing so at hand. He only survived by closing his eyes and recalling what he had known in the past. He had to live on memories. He thought of his past freedom, and regretted that he had not consciously savored it more intensely. It was only in looking back that he realized how great had been his enjoyment of life and freedom at the time.

His thoughts were morose. In his mind's eye he saw only darkness and gloom. "Regions of terror, doleful shades, where peace and rest can never dwell, hope never comes..." were the mental images he shared with John Milton. /1

/1   Phrases educed from Milton's "Paradise Lost"

70

That was when some of his friends were able to arrange plans with sympathetic prison guards to bring Jacques some brushes and paints and blank canvases. Perhaps Jacques could make some portraits from memory, or put on canvas his impressions of the dank, cold, forbidding, redoubtable, immutable, adamantine, slimy walls of the prison. He needed something -- anything -- to help him fill in the hours; something to help him cling to life.

Jacques received the equipment with but little interest or excitement at first. His spirit was downtrodden after months of imprisonment. He felt he must have lost any skill he ever possessed. Furthermore, he had no interesting subjects like dukes or generals or princesses to pose for him. His only ray of light and life in this dismal cell squeezed in through a tiny window covered with bars and an iron grating.

In spite of his initial lethargy, and because he was not pressed for time right then, he began mixing some paints. The smell seemed to touch his inner reflexes and stimulated a renewed interest in creating something on canvas once again. A Pavlovian response.

So he did it. He made a beautiful painting like none he had ever done before or since. All of David's other great paintings were people and portraits. This was a landscape, the only landscape painting he ever made. The only other known landscapes of any sort to have come from the hand of Jacques David are some pencil sketches of the Tuscan hills and seacoast made during his year in Italy.

This was a new first for Jacques, this one-and-only item. It was an oil painting, 55cm by 65cm, in full color, of the Luxembourg Gardens in spring, filled with budding green foliage of the sycamore trees, brightly colored flowers, bees and butterflies spreading pollen and fresh growth all about, gently washed by warm sunshine pouring down from Heaven giving new life and energy to the earth below.

It is what he saw, looking through the bars of his prison window.

THE END

Epilogue

Some critics have described this painting, the only full landscape known to have been painted by Jacques Louis David, as being a precursor to the Barbizon School. It even suggested the coming Impressionist movement 75 years later. The painting is now hanging in the Musée d'Orsay, on the bank of the Seine, about half a mile from the Luxembourg Gardens and the prison where it was painted. Go see it the next time you are in Paris.

THE FINAL END

What Do You Say to a Naked Woman?

I once lived in Copenhagen for a couple of years, and you may not know it, but the Scandinavians are sun-worshipers. That's right, sun-worshipers. There is so little sunshine that far north that most of the Danes and Swedes and others try to get as much sun as they can, at every opportunity, whenever and wherever possible.

I have also been to Spain, and was there many years ago when Franco was in power. Franco was the national authority and the guardian of his people's Victorian morals as well as most other aspects of their lives. There was a popular story of the French woman who came to Spain on a holiday visit. She found the Spanish beaches on the Bay of Biscay much to her liking, and in a most natural fashion exposed her skin -- a good bit of it -- to the warm caresses of the Iberian sunshine. She was wearing a two-piece bathing suit of a sufficiently skimpy design to qualify for the newly-invented term "Bikini." According to the story, as told by the dirty old men who met regularly for lunch to gorge themselves while swapping lies and risqué tales, the young *demoiselle* had stretched out on the sand at San Sebastian and was enjoying the bright *soleil de l'après-midi* when a member of the local *Policía* or *Guardia Civil,* charged with maintaining public order, propriety, and decorum, sneaked up to her and rapped her on the shoulder with his ubiquitous riding crop or nightstick.

73

"Señorita, don't you know that eet ees against zee law for a woman to wear a two-piece bathing suit on a public beach een España?"

"It is?"

"Sí, señorita, eet ees. Even here een zee Basque Count Tree"

"Oh, pardón. I am very sorry. Which piece would you like for me to remove?"

Then of course the old men would laugh like crazy even though they had all heard the story a million times before.

My story today involves a sailboat trip my wife and I made one weekend along the southwestern coast of Sweden.

* * * * *

It was a beautiful sunny afternoon in mid-August. We had been sailing all morning from Copenhagen, north, up the Øresund into the Kattegat between Sweden and Norway. We had just anchored our boat in a cove on the lovely island of Anholt and were relaxing on the isolated sandy beach. In Scandinavia, clothing is definitely optional or completely absent on isolated sandy beaches, and, indeed, on busy suburban beaches and urban parks as well. With the short sunny summer season, every minute and square inch of sun must be seized and used to full advantage. After living in Denmark for a year, I found it easy to slip out of my old habits and customs and into the local customs -- out of my bathing suit and into the sunshine or the ocean, -- when opportunities offered themselves. This was one such an opportunity.

So there I was, naked as the original of Michelangelo's "David." I was going in and out of the ocean with aplomb, when a beautiful Scandinavian twin of Anita Ekberg's /1 came strolling along the water's edge, like young Lochinvar out of the West, silhouetted against the late afternoon sun.

I could see she wasn't wearing much -- at first I thought only a fuzzy white bikini bottom, almost transparent. Then I realized it was absolutely nothing, only the vestigial outline left by the sun where a bikini bottom had once been. Of course, a gentleman would never focus his attention on the bottom half of a woman's bikini, regardless of how skimpy and enticing the "swim-wear" designers had endeavored to make it. The gentleman's attentions may have already been seized by other attractive elements farther north, revealing themselves in all their beauty -- her golden *chevelure,* her sparkling blue eyes, the clear skin of her cheek bones, and the inchoate smile of two lovely lips, not to mention the curve of her shoulders and the shapely prominence of her collarbones.

Whenever I see a woman with a lovely neckline like that, I recall one of the old songs my mother used to get all of us kids to sing on our summer evening walks down

---

/1 Anita Ekberg (1931-2015), Miss Sweden 1950, was a spectacular actress, famous for her rôle in Federico Fellini's 1960 film, LA DOLCE VITA, "one of the most critically acclaimed movies of all time." (Wikipedia)

the Howard Gap Road, "Swing Low, Sweet Chariot." My friend Bobby Billings in the eighth grade said Swing Low Sweet Chariot was the name of a Brassière company in Montgomery, Alabama, that was bought out later by Maidenform. I never checked the veracity of his story, but accepted it. Anyway, I think the name is fitting, so to speak, and the image has stayed with me over the years.

I had been on nude beaches before; even Brighton, England has one. But somehow, at Brighton, where there were a lot of people together, all one crowd, enjoying the sun, you didn't notice the others. If they reminded you of anything, it was the phrase "No Sex, Please, We're British," which I think was made into a Broadway play some years ago. But this time this person was extraordinary, and she was alone, and she was coming right toward me on the isolated beach on Anholt. I would have to say something; it would be impolite not to.

She was getting nearer. It looked as though we were on a collision course. She kept coming, and the closer she came, the more prominent her curves seemed to appear, like the headlights of a distant Volvo convertible approaching through the morning mist. I had to think of something to say. A menu of possibilities flashed across my mind. (See Attachment for list of my thoughts on possible salutations.) It was not going to be easy. She kept getting closer. I had to think fast. I couldn't turn away and run; I had to say something. The gentleman should always speak first. The trouble is that everything that came to my mind seemed either too bold or not bold enough. Oh my, what a pickle it was, albeit a sweet pickle. A sweet gherkin there: this beautiful Scandinavian goddess getting nearer

76

and nearer, with her radiance and swinging charm, clearly visible, almost tangible, before my eyes. Tangible? Oh, my! I tried to blink, but that would have been difficult, and perhaps cowardly as well.

Now she was just a few steps away from me, in all her God-given frontal glory. And she was still coming closer. I felt my own body wanting to respond. Would she notice the effect she was having on me? How could she fail to? Does pride or shame go with a spontaneous physical response? She was naked and I was too, I now realized. Would I embarrass her? Would she embarrass me? Oh yes, yes. A little embarrassment is ever so much sweeter than indifference. Embarrassment and speech are the two characteristics that distinguish human beings from the apes and other lesser animals. Would she, like women from time immemorial, through the ages, enjoy knowing the physical effect her radiance has upon members of the opposite gender, especially those of handsome young men, like me?

I think her lips were open as she came almost to body contact, although at that moment my eyes had dropped, not exactly from embarrassment, but because of a combination of shyness, admiration, awe, excitement, and curiosity. But it was the moment for words, not action. I had to break the ice somehow. I could not let this God-sent creature, this Venus Emerging From The Half-Shell, this remarkable combination of Anita Ekberg and Liv Ullmann rolled into one (if you can imagine that) -- pass me by, thinking I had not properly admired her or possibly that I had not even noticed her. (She did not seem to be a woman who wanted to go unnoticed.)

77

I tried to open my lips when her own lovely lips were just a few feet away from mine. Inside my mind I was rummaging about, rapidly culling through the list of possible greetings I might offer her, but it seemed an almost impossible task to actually get my mouth around the appropriate words. Even if I ever did get the right words into my mouth I was not sure I would be able to get them out, audibly. Nothing in my mental list of possible things to say seemed quite *à propos.*

At the last moment, as the salty aroma of her sun-dried, golden-blond hair wafted over me in passing, I did manage to get the words "Hello there" into my mouth, but, unfortunately, they stuck in my throat. Her own lips parted sightly, as though she were ready and waiting to respond to any overture I could conjure up. But alas, I was mute.

And so the vision passed. I had missed my chance to engage the lovely curvacious mermaid in conversation, and she passed me by. My moment had evaporated. Gone with the Wind.

I would like to think the sweet thing realized I *did* notice, and that she was pleased to know I was enjoying the sight of her, swaying gently from right to left, like a lighthouse calling attention to the beauties of nature. Perhaps she enjoyed our near-encounter almost as much as I did. Yes, I would like to think so.

Finally, the rear view was also worth another glance: you couldn't help admiring her shoulder blades as she continued on her way eastward, rhythmically swinging along the water's edge, fading into the distance.

There it was: the lovely end of a lovely day.

THE END

THOUGHTS OF WHAT YOU MIGHT SAY
ON A NUDE BEACH
TO A
GORGEOUS CURVACEOUS
SUN-WORSHIPING VENUS
WITH LOTS OF BEAUTIFUL SKIN
NAKED
SUDDENLY RIGHT IN FRONT OF YOU

"Excuse me, have you got the time?"

"Haven't I seen you before somewhere?"

"Can you change a twenty?"

"Do you speak Italian?"

"Have you been swimming?"

"Hi there. I am an American. Where are you from?"

"Do you like volleyball?"

"Jag älskar dej."

"I like your hairdo."

"Excuse me, have you got a match?

"Do you know where I can mail a letter?"

"You look like Anita Ekberg, with your swinging... stride, and your pair of lovely long legs, right there, underneath you."

80

"Can you tell me which way it is to the ocean?"

"I see some clouds over there. Do you think we are going to need our rain-clothes?"

"You look a lot like a nurse I had when I was a baby."

"Excuse my casual attire." (I was naked.)

"Do you know what time the sun sets?"

"Do you live around here?"

"Hi there! My name is Percival."

"I'll share my towel with you if you'd like."

"Would you care to stop and have a sandwich with my wife and me?"

"Do you like Renoir? Rubens?"

"What kind of sunscreen do you use?"

"Would you like some help putting it on?"

"My camera doesn't work. Do you know where I can get it fixed?"

"Have you done your Christmas shopping yet?"

"Do you come here often?"

"Does your mother know you're out?"

"Is there any place around here where they sell bathing suits? My wife forgot hers."

"Do you like sunshine?"

THE FINAL END

Opening Day

"Boy oh boy, are you two guys gonna catch it!" said Hank Allister, one of our classmates. Hank was there with Bart Finney, and Gordon Lockwood, but he was talking to Kim and me.

And he was right, and we did catch it, because of the unfair, stupid, deceitful world we live in.

Kim and I were fifteen years old. I remember it was only a few days after my birthday, which is in March. Hank and Bart were about that age too; we were all in the ninth grade at school.

* * * * *

Kelvern Mimford was my best friend (he had shortened his name to Kim for daily use.) The two of us were rather different in a number of ways, and maybe that is why we fitted together and got along so well. Kim was more gregarious than I was, somewhat bigger, more athletic, better looking, and a "bigger man on campus." I was quieter, more introverted I guess, slower with the girls, more studious, and got better grades.

There was one thing we did have in common though: we both loved baseball. Kim was a pretty good athlete himself. I could run as fast as he could, but he could throw the ball a lot harder, and hit the ball farther, than I could,

83

and he could talk baseball and a lot of other things much faster and better than I could. He knew all the stats, the pitchers' ERA's, batters' averages, home-runs, strikeouts, walks, steals, etc. He was sort of a contemporary God to me, right here on earth, where I still was at the time.

About the only thing I could do that he couldn't do was math. I helped him through school with his math, even if we cheated a little in the process. In later years I have read that there has been a great deal of cheating going on in schools and colleges all over the country, and it sounds like a lot more than the little bit of cheating we did. Kim had to cheat a little to get through and keep up his average, and I had to help him cheat in order to keep up my position as a buddy and cohort of his, maybe his principal buddy. He needed me, but I needed him too. He was my connection with cool people and society outside of the world of nerds.

He didn't like his name, Mimford, which I guess came from a Scottish ancestor, or "Scots" ancestor, as they prefer to be called -- those still alive anyway. He didn't like Kelvern much better; he thought it sounded more like a girl's name. At first he changed it to Kevin, and then to Kim. If anybody ever teased him about it they got a punch in the nose or found themselves in a fight, which Kim, now being quite experienced in such matters, usually won.

Kim was quite an inventive fellow -- inventor of pranks, that is. There were a number of clever things he used to do, or taught me how do do.

The first bit of Kim's chicanery that I remember was his trick of making a free call from a public pay phone. He

84

would put his nickel in, dial zero, and say, "Operator, I got the wrong number; I wanted OLiver 27five9," stressing one of the digits to get his idea across. "Sorry, Sir." The nickel would come down into the coin return cup and the call would go through free of charge. If he had to make two or three calls and was afraid of getting the same operator, he knew how to make a penny work for a nickel. If you spun it with the blade of your pocket knife as it was going into the slot, half the time it would jump into the nickel channel and connect your call. Sometimes it took two or three tries to get enough spin on it to make it work; otherwise the penny came back in the coin return cup. When it worked, you saved four cents on a call.

Another way he could save money was always to ask for a transfer slip when he got on a city bus or streetcar, whether he needed it or not. A transfer slip was always torn across the bottom to show the last hour of its validity. The date was shown at the top. If you saved the transfer slip you got this morning, and combined it with the tail of yesterday afternoon's transfer slip, and held the two pieces carefully together, you had a free ride this afternoon. It may sound complicated but it was simple, and it would save you ten cents busfare after school.

There was another clever trick of Kim's that never made him any money, but gave him some chuckles, I guess. One time he went into each of the toilet stalls in the men's room in the basement of the Chevy Chase Hot Shoppe, locked the door, and then climbed out over the top, or squeezed out under the bottom of the door, in great glee. I remember telling him he shouldn't have done that, but I did admire his aplomb. I even went back later and crawled under to open at least one of the stalls. After all, someone might come in with an emergency.

But I got him once though. It was in church one Sunday morning. We each had a quarter for the offering. "Give me your quarter," he said, "I'll put in the plate with mine." I knew his effort to display unwonted generosity would not fool God, so I said, "No, you give me *your* quarter and I'll put it in with mine. I'm closer." (I meant closer to the aisle, not closer to God. I wouldn't go that far.) "I'll flip you for it," he said. So we flipped for the privilege of putting in the two quarters, and I won. When the plate came around, I put the two quarters in and then nonchalantly passed the plate along to Kim, next to me at the inside end of the row. He was speechless, nonplussed, there with no quarter, helplessly looking for a moment at the plate in front of him in mild horror. You wouldn't have talked at a time like that, even if you could have thought of anything to say. After embarrassing him for three or four seconds I "realized" that Kim had chosen not to contribute to the offering that morning, and passed the plate back along the row to the usher patiently waiting in the aisle. It's about the only time I ever got ahead of him outside of the classroom.

Kim had to keep me his friend because I would explain our math homework to him and let him cheat off me a little on some of the tests. He always sat right behind me where he could look over my shoulder, when necessary. Not all the time, just sometimes. "Write large," he used to say in a muffled whisper.

Later on, Kim must have had a talk with God about our wayward behavior, or his anyway. The two of them apparently negotiated some satisfactory arrangement, because Kim eventually became an Episcopal priest. So you might say he paid for his sins, but at a rather severe price, it seems to me. Meanwhile, in my own life all I ever got to be was a functionary in the Foreign Ministry, or State Department, as it was called domestically.

* * * * *

Big League Baseball in those days was a daytime sport; night games had not yet gotten popular and were still very rare. The beginning of the baseball season every spring was an exciting time. Opening Day was particularly exciting, especially in Washington, D.C., where we lived. It traditionally meant the Washington Senators' playing the Philadelphia Athletics, or maybe the New York Yankees, at Griffith Stadium. It would be the only game in the country played that day; the other teams in both leagues began their baseball schedules the following day. So it was a big deal at Griffith Stadium in Washington. There was usually some high-ranking dignitary who came and threw out the first ball, sometimes the Vice President or the President himself.

* * * * *

Kim's parents had a bigger house than my parents did, and Kim's room had an extra bed. I would sometimes go over to his house for the afternoon, where we would play catch or take turns pitching and batting in his backyard, as well as try other games. Sometimes, with my parents' permission of course, I would stay and spend the night and go on to school with him the next day.

"Tomorrow's Opening Day," he said one evening in early April. "The Senators are playing the Philadelphia Athletics. Let's go to the game."

"It starts at one o'clock," I observed, with a doubtful voice. "We'd never make it. We would miss the first six innings unless we cut out from school early, and that would be pretty obvious."

"No, leaving school early wouldn't be a very good idea," agreed Kim in his wisdom, as his mind raced ahead. "Everyone would see what we were doing." Then his eyes lit up and his whole countenance brightened noticeably. "We'll just skip the whole day."

"You mean play hooky?"

"If that's what you want to call it."

So that's what we called it, and that's what we did. We decided to play hooky.

Without telling anyone of our plans, we left his house the next morning at the usual time. We took the bus that always went by our school, but we didn't get off; we stayed on until we got downtown, near the stadium. That gave us two or three three hours to kill, so we walked around the rest of the morning, got a couple of hotdogs, and then went over to the ballpark around noon. We were free as birds.

Larks. Excellerated. We were keyed up with the double excrement of our nautical behaviour in skidding classeys without persimmon plus the thrall of boing perhaps the only skids from cool to see the Senders and the Atheletes go to it on opining day.

So you can imagine how surprised we were to see Hank Allister and Bart Finney already there. As I started to ask them whether they were playing hooky too, they preëmpted me, jeering almost in unison, "Boy oh boy, are you two guys gonna catch it!"

"What are you talking about?" we politely inquired.

"They had Assembly at school this morning, nine o'clock, and said that anybody who wanted to go to the Game could be excused after the second period. They took a rollcall, and you weren't there. You're going to catch it," they repeated, with laughs and sniggers. "You two guys are playing hooky," they added, in unnecessary explanation.

Yes, we knew that. But we didn't know that anybody else knew it. What a low-down, deceitful school we went to. They could have made an announcement yesterday or the day before, instead of tricking us like this and making it look as though Kim and I were the ones doing wrong.

* * * * *

The next day we went to school in the normal way, with straight faces and our hands in our pockets, as nonchalant as the "Who, me?" kid with the happy face. In the normal way, we thought, but a normal day it was not to be. It

89

seems the whole school was lying in *guet-apens*, ready and waiting to put us in stocks and throw eggs at us (figuratively speaking, unfortunately).

"Oh boy, are you guys going to catch it!" we heard from all sides round, as soon as we got on the school grounds. Yes, we had heard that before. We had little peace, and no rest at all, from the moment we arrived. At the first class break the Headmaster's secretary, Miss Nasenstein, descended upon us as we were coming out of math class. Not surprisingly she said, rather more loudly than necessary, and to the glee of all our classmates within earshot, "Doctor Streitaufreisen wants to see you in his office." Streitaufreisen, our percipient Headmaster, was a Doctor of Divinity, and therefore he had every right to put "Doctor" in front of his name at every opportunity.

"Now you're going to catch it," was the friendly advice we heard once again, those familiar words, coming in a torrent of jeers from our sympathetic classmates.

And they were right. And we did.

THE ORIGINAL END

Epilogue

At this point I should tell you something about our Headmaster, Doctor Streitaufreisen, and his relationship with Kelvern Mimford, otherwise known as Kim. They already knew each other; they had met before. They were both hard-headed, refractory, self-willed types, but in many ways they were quite different. It was sort of a church

90

school that we went to, and our Headmaster was an Episcopal priest and scholar, a conservative traditionalist who was intolerant, overbearing, imperious, unforgiving, and always right. Not only right but self-righteous as well.

Kim however was willful and renitent, and he chaffed under restrictions and regulations that he thought were unnecessary or trivial. For instance, the Headmaster didn't like the slowly descending sideburns that Kim was carefully cultivating as he strove toward adulthood. "Get 'em up, get 'em up," he would tell Kim, simultaneously flicking his index finger to stress what he meant by "up." Kim would "comply" by trimming them a quarter of an inch. Not enough. "Get 'em up," the Headmaster would say again the next time he saw him. So their little war went on. And Kim's necktie. We had to wear proper jackets and ties in the proper little church school, and Kim subtly proclaimed his individuality and resistance by wearing improper, even outlandish if not garish, painted neckties in splashy colors, some with interesting pulchritudinous cartoon artwork out of sight on the reverse side. Nowhere did it say in the school regulations that our neckties had to be conservative, sedate, or even somber, so that furnished more fuel for Kim's recusant struggle against authority.

Although I did not realize it at the time, Kim's decision to play hooky was, in part, an expression of his ongoing anti-establishmentarianism struggle. Kim was of course the one who decided that we should play hooky, although I happily considered myself an integral part of the plot. Old Streitaufreisen wasn't born yesterday, and he had sufficiently penetrating powers of insight to realize that the brains and driving force behind the hooky game came from

Kim and not from me. "It came from both of us," I forcefully protested, more concerned to preserve my image as Kim's faithful crony and co-conspirator by sharing the blame than to acknowledge that my own pure and wimpy heart and soul could never have conceived of such a dastardly deed. I was proud of my allegiance to Kim's rebellious behavior, and preferred to suffer fully in collusion with him. Please, I must be equally accused of our sinful scheming. Friendship and loyalty are more important than honesty and regulations. But I didn't fool Streitaufreisen. He seized upon the realization that it was Kim's plan, accused me of being Kim's personal myrmidon, whatever that is, and much to my chagrin upbraided me for being duped and for "letting Kim put a hook in my nose."

Those were his words, and they stung like fire, and because the metaphor was accurate they hurt even more. "No, no," I insisted, "it was both of us. We both had the idea."

My only consolation came by my receiving the same number of demerits that Kim got -- six, I think it was. Perhaps Streitaufreisen didn't realize how completely he could have demolished me if he had given me only, say, four demerits, while Kim was getting six.

Meanwhile Kim was of course catching Hellish opprobrium and fulminations straight from the dragon's mouth too. Flagrantly wayward conduct. Peccant violation of school regulations. Execrable disregard for parents' investment in your education. Unconscionable setting of bad examples for others. Odious misrepresentation of intentions. Heinous corruption of morals. Blatant succumbing to the enticements of the Devil. Ah, yes, the Devil. Kim and the Headmaster. Each saw the Devil in the other. Kim saw the Devil, or his tactics, in the way the Headmaster treated him, with the Headmaster's cloaking himself in the protective coloring of his priestly robes and backwards collar.

But in the end Kim fought fire with fire, and ultimately got back at the Headmaster and the entire unfair system. After college and a two-year stint in the army, Kim went to seminary and soon thereafter got ordained as an Episcopal priest himself.

Nobody on earth was going to tell *him* what to do.

THE FINAL END

True Love

"Is this seat taken?" she asked unnecessarily, with an impish smile in her blue eyes.

"It is now," I said, both surprised and pleased, as the lovely young woman slid in beside me on the chairlift. It was a bright January day of skiing at a little slope called "Homewood" on Lake Tahoe near Squaw Valley.

Then a most amazing thing happened. She looked at me and I at her, and, close as we were together in the chair, we moved our heads and noses slightly closer to each other, looking mostly into each other's eyes. Then, for no good reason that we knew of, we kept on until our lips were almost together. No words beyond the initial exchange. Somehow our lips touched. It was a kiss -- I suppose you would call it a kiss -- very light, cool, transient, ephemeral, nugatory, unplanned, pointless, forgettable. Why we kissed, complete unknowns as we were, out of sight of any other human beings, I don't know, and she didn't know either, she said later. It just happened, on a cold day on the ski slopes. But the ice was broken, so to speak.

We skied down together a couple of times and rode up together a couple of times. She told me her name was Jane Fontenelli and that her number was in the Menlo Park telephone book. I live in Mountain View, not far from Menlo Park, so I said I would give her a call, and that maybe we could see each other again sometime, not really thinking it likely. She said she would remember me because my name is Dick Anderson and she thought "Dick and Jane" had a certain ring to it, like ice cream and cake. Or maybe scotch and soda. Then we split and went back to the people we had come with. Frankly, I never expected to see her again. But as it turned out, I didn't forget her; I did remember her name. And I remember that I remembered it because it sounded sort of like Jane Mansfield and Jane Russell.

I had come to Lake Tahoe with an old friend, a lady friend of sorts, named Clarissa Moore, who only skied a little. She was back at the lodge having a glass or two of *glühwein* while I was still on the slopes meeting Jane. Clarissa had been in one of my classes when I was in Graduate School at Stanford some years before, and knew a lot of my friends and associates. We started going together, after a fashion, three or four years ago, because to tell the truth, many of the people we knew just expected us to, and neither of us had anybody else on the horizon. She had been married when she was only nineteen, but it didn't last a year. After that she went back to finish her schooling and was now some kind of an executive in the corporate world. When, in due course, she started to consider the idea of a new man in her life, she saw that I seemed available, and I guess she decided I would do; I would be her next, and life-long, companion. And she would marry me some day. So we have been going together since then. I like Clarissa, I like her fine, although we have never been officially engaged. I wasn't in any hurry to get married, but I wasn't particularly interested in any other women either.

* * * * *

A couple of weeks after that weekend at Tahoe, I looked up Jane Fontenelli in the phone book, out of curiosity, and telephoned her. She said she did remember me, adding sweetly that she had been hoping I might call. We decided to meet for lunch the following Thursday at a place we both knew in Palo Alto. I had no ulterior motives or designs. Not then. It was just lunch, which I probably would have been having anyway. I liked her pleasant chit-chat and her company. That seemed to be enough. But sometimes an attraction between people may develop of its own accord, when no one is watching out for it, or planning for it. I guess that's what happened with Jane and me. I certainly found her appealing, with her outgoing, fresh nature and pretty smile. I enjoyed my lunch with her. The next week we had lunch again. Simple. Pleasant.

I could get fond of this Jane I thought, although by then I had been going with Clarissa for almost four years. Clarissa was dependable, and was All Right, and I wasn't looking for a new romance in my life. But it happened anyway. I even felt like writing a "Dear Abby" letter asking whether I should stick with what I had, a reliable woman, tried and true, with whom I had developed a relationship that was well founded in habit and routine -- or yield to a new passion and excitement that had entered my life casually, randomly, inexplicably and spontaneously, of its own accord.

Jane and I by now were beginning to feel a strong attraction for each other, including physical attraction. It seems that Jane had lost her boyfriend a while ago, to another man, as it were.

My long-standing affair with Clarissa could have been perhaps best described as "so-so."

Jane was more enticing than Clarissa, reminding me somewhat of that other Jane -- Jane Mansfield the movie star -- whose attributes I had always admired. And now I seemed to be falling for this Jane. I realized that, in truth, she and I were better suited for each other than Clarissa and I were, in spite of our satisfactory years together.

Now it so happened that one weekend in early March, when Clarissa was in Los Angeles visiting her parents, I decided to take another few days on the ski slopes. Not to go alone, I asked Jane, in a very polite fashion, if she would like to go along too. "Yes, I think that might be rather nice," she demurely replied in a very ladylike manner.

Well, we went back to Homewood, and what we did mostly was ski. I think each of us was afraid of scaring the other off by possibly coming on too fast, so we skied, and talked, and drank a little wine together, but nothing much more.

When the time came for us to leave, we kissed, lightly at first, but because it tasted so good, we kissed again and pressed our bodies together a little.

"I didn't know you were interested in this sort of thing," I said. "I didn't know you were interested in romance."

"Oh, but I am, I love romance. Since my boyfriend left me six months ago, I have been hoping to find another, Dick," said Jane.

98

"You should have told me sooner, Jane," said Dick -- said I. "Now it's time for us to head back."

"I tried to tell you, but you didn't seem interested."

On the drive back, with my elated spirits, I told her that I was indeed interested -- that she was mistaken. "I thought I was being cool and casual," I said, firmly asseverating that I really was in love with her. I even suggested that I would be glad to stay the night at her place sometime so we could "reminisce about our lovely weekend of skiing together," and get to know each other even better as our love continued to grow.

"But you have Clarissa."

"If you want to know the truth, ever since I first met you on the chairlift, you are the only one I have thought about that way. You got me excited, looking at you, and remembering you, and thinking of you, and I got so worked up I had to go back to Clarissa to let off steam. Clarissa was just a means for me to let off the pressure you had built up in me. Since then I have always been thinking of you the whole time I have ever been with her. Honest. I even pretended it was you. At least sometimes I did... And now I have Clarissa around my neck, claiming she is pregnant and I don't know what all... You have to help me."

"Pregnant? Oh my God! How could... "

"I don't think she really *is* pregnant. It's just a trick of hers."

"And how am I supposed to help you?"

"You have to knock her off. It's the only way."

"Knock her off? WHAT! You mean murder? Like kill her or something?"

"Yes, of course. People die all the time. Look at the *San Francisco Chronicle* any day of the week. But if I were the one to knock her off, not only would I be the prime suspect, but also they would know it was premeditated, and I would really get the ax. But you could do it in a fit of jealous rage, a justifiable murder -- you know, justifiable rage. You could be in a fit of temporary insanity on seeing your beloved stolen right out from under your nose by another woman. The worst that they could charge you with would probably be manslaughter, but with any luck at all they might call it justifiable homicide and drop the charges entirely and let you off Scot free. The courts are always easier on women than they are on men. Anyway, everybody knows that a woman scorned usually goes out of her mind. Just claim temporary insanity. You didn't know what you were doing. You shouldn't have any trouble doing that. It would be easy."

"I'm going to have to think about that one."

"Don't think too much, or else it will be premeditated, and that would be bad."

So Jane did it. She knocked off Clarissa. She called me to give me the good news, and I thanked her profusely, but you may not be surprised to learn that I had bad dreams that night.

100

When I woke up the next morning, I looked over to the other side of the bed and Clarissa wasn't there. I got to thinking, and it came to me that I had made a mistake. I should have gotten Clarissa to knock off Jane. I realized then that it was Clarissa I loved... the one I really loved... my true love.

Alas, too late.

THE END

Short Stories Encore

102

My Suggestion Is

His name was Felipe Maldonado, or maybe that was just an alias. He wasn't a bad guy -- not all bad anyway -- but he was in a bit of a jam. "What am I going to do?" he wailed, with a heavy Mexican accent.

"My advice is..." the consular officer started in.

Although the officer knew Maldonado wasn't going to like what he had to tell him, Maldonado's choices were limited, which is to say, down to about one, unless suicide could be considered another choice. But Maldonado wasn't that type; he had survived tough conditions growing up poor in Mexico, and he could survive this too, somehow. But the American Consul knew his words would bring no joy to this *vaquero* from South of the Border.

*   *   *   *   *

In recent weeks and months there has been a lot of talk about US immigration policy and about the many Hispanic foreigners living in the United States illegally. You would think that for many years our government must have had no immigration control at all, or just didn't care, which was not exactly true.

Furthermore, many, if not most, of the foreigners illegally living in the United States may have entered the country *legally* and then overstayed, violating the conditions of their admission. So a fence wouldn't have done much good.

In the old days there were no national quotas for immigrants coming to the United States from Western Hemisphere countries. All that they needed to immigrate was a good record, good morals, good health, good behavior, a good job prospect, and enough patience to carry them through the official procedures.

Of course, there are a lot of people of Mexican ancestry with Hispanic names living in California and Arizona and the rest of the Great Southwest. Most of them speak Spanish, although many of them never immigrated to the United States. They are the descendents of the people who were already living throughout that vast region when we acquired it from Mexico in 1848, after the Mexican War.

For much of the twentieth century we had established a quota system for aspiring immigrants from other countries. It was based upon the estimated proportion in our population (as it existed in 1910 or 1890) of Americans with ethnic or linguistic or cultural origins from the various foreign countries. Our immigration law was called the National Origins Act of 1924, whose concept was to maintain, essentially unchanged, the proportionate cultural and racial mix of the people who had settled this land and made this country great.

However, there was one big exception to this immigration policy. Stemming from the days of the Monroe Doctrine, there had developed in the United States a different attitude toward Western Hemisphere countries. We viewed citizens of these countries as significantly different from citizens of Europe and the rest of the world. People born in the Western Hemisphere were Good Guys. With our Revolutionary War we separated ourselves from England, and, with our approval and sometimes with our support, other Western Hemisphere countries also separated themselves from their Eastern Hemisphere motherlands that had colonized them and dominated them for centuries. We viewed the other Western Hemisphere countries as our brothers-in-arms, Good Guys, and our early immigration laws had no quota restriction on immigration of citizens from Western Hemisphere countries into the United States.

There were some other restrictions, however. Naturally, we did not want habitual criminals or people with contagious diseases to enter. The list of qualifications (and disqualifications) to immigrate went on considerably longer. Disqualifications also included: the likelihood to become a public charge (by not having a job prospect), plans to overthrow the government or cause civil unrest, or intent to engage in prostitution or drug-running or any other naughty or illegal behavior. Indeed, the term "having no visible means of support" became a euphemism for prostitution.

At the time of this story, our government had already begun to feel that unrestricted immigration might become excessive and hence undesirable, even if it did come from countries of our hemisphere that hated European empire-builders as much as we Americans did. Accordingly, our authorities who were responsible for applying the aforementioned qualitative restrictions were tacitly encouraged to apply them rigorously in an unofficial effort toward some small degree of quantity control as well.

The immigration procedures became longer and more involved. Papers, documents, and red tape led to months and sometimes even years of waiting time. Accordingly, Mexicans and others desiring to live in the United States felt an increased pressure to bypass the time-consuming and parlous immigration process. The simplest way to do so, besides wading across the Rio Grande in the dark of night, was to enter with a temporary visa -- as a tourist or visitor or businessman or student for instance -- and then overstay the terms of admission and melt into the crowd.

Our consular officers in Mexico and elsewhere were well aware of this ruse, and were under instructions to assiduously assess the intentions of a prospective visitor, or any other "non-immigrant," and to refuse to issue an entry visa if it appeared likely that he might violate his conditions of admission and stay on to live in the United States -- that is to say, as an immigrant.

* * * * *

It was in the spring of 1959 that Felipe Maldonado applied for a B-2 temporary-visitor visa at one of our consulates on the Mexican border. His application was refused.

In Señor Maldonado's case, not only US laws applied, but a few Mexican laws applied as well. Clearly Mexican laws and law-enforcement officers were not involved with the enforcement of US immigration policies, nor were they much concerned about "emigration" from Mexico. However, Mexican officials did devote great attention to mundane matters like the enforcement of Mexican tax laws and the collection of tariffs. Automobiles imported into Mexico faced high tariff duties, often virtually doubling the price of a car. Economic pressures being what they are, it looked like good business to somehow bring a car into Mexico as a visitor and sell it illegally. Tourists were allowed to drive their cars into Mexico, but were expected to take them out when they left the country. In fact, because some naughty tourists could not be trusted, it became the law that the vehicle had to leave the country with the departure of the tourist. Therefore and thereafter, the visa or "tourist card" with which a foreign visitor entered Mexico was invariably over-stamped "ENTRÓ CON AUTOMÓVIL" in giant letters -- "Entered with Automobile." The entry permit was for both a man and his car, and was their exit permit as well. One could not leave the country without the other upon the termination of the visit.

Now our friend Felipe Maldonado was a bright boy for his size, and he got the bright idea of having an American tourist bring a nice new American car into Mexico and then die or disappear or vanish into thin air as though he never existed. "Yes, that's it!" thought Maldonado. If he never existed they couldn't make him leave. And he, Maldonado, would have to take care of the car, now in Mexico, without an owner. Well, he knew how to do that.

Maldonado had some friends and relatives living in Corpus Christi, Texas, where he thought he himself might want to live someday, but for now he would settle for making some money in Mexico -- and he had an idea.

He was able to get a visitor visa good for one entry from a generous American consul at a border post who believed his promise that he would return to Mexico at the end of his visit, after only a few days.

He went to Corpus where the first thing he did was to get a Texas State fishing license at a convenience store that was authorized to sell hunting and fishing licenses as well as rods and guns. That was easy: no ID required, just $10 and a smile, and good for the season. Name on the fishing license...?   any name you want -- "Joe Aguirre" for instance.

Joe Aguirre was a name Maldonado had heard of;   it belonged to a neighbor who lived down the street from the house of Joe's brother-in-law in Corpus Christi. So now Maldonado had an address as well as a name. Might be helpful to have, if he had to show something upon buying the car he wanted. An address could be useful.

Maldonado went to AutoNation Chevrolet Cadillac, the biggest General Motors dealer in Corpus Christi, and bought a new 1958 Chevrolet Bel Air sedan for $2,899, loaded. Eight cylinders, two-tone green and white -- two-thirds of the colors of the Mexican flag. Hydromatic transmission, back-up lights, radio, power steering -- the whole bit. It would sell well in Mexico. He showed his fishing license for ID, gave the address of this Joe Aguirre on his brother-in-law's street, paid in cash, and set off for

Mexico. He drove carefully, observing all speed limits and attentively stopping at every red light and octagonal sign he saw.

He sang mariachi songs happily all the way to the border-crossing point he had chosen, 175 miles up the river.

Let them put "*Entró con auto*" on his tourist card. Joe Aguirre could die and go to heaven for all he cared. His plan was perfect.

Now some of the Mexican customs officials may be dumb, but they are not stupid. This Felipe Maldonado fellow, wearing dusty cowboy boots and patched blue jeans, did not seem consistent with the type of friends the American owner of such a beautiful, shiny new two-tone Chevrolet Bel-Air automobile ought to have. They asked him a few more questions.

Maldonado said Joe Aguirre would be coming to Mexico for his vacation, but was pressed for time right now. He explained that Aguirre planned to fly to Mexico City to pick up his car and then drive down to Cuernavaca and Taxco and maybe Acapulco for a few days' holiday; he would then drive back to Corpus. Maldonado was just saving his busy friend a couple of days by bringing the car on ahead. Doing him a favor, that's all. He made it sound like a good story.

But you can't fool all the people all the time, and the Mexican Customs officials at the border told Maldonado that the owner had to be the driver, or at least a passenger present in the car, for it to come into Mexico. "Go back and get the owner to drive in with you," they told him.

Maldonado drove back across the bridge to the US side and explained that the Mexican authorities would not let him bring the car into Mexico without the owner, and that he had to take the car back to the owner in Corpus Christi. But now the US immigration authorities would not let him pass. "Your visa was for a single entry," they observed. "Now it's expired -- you have already used it. Go to the US Consulate and get another visa," they told him.

But the consular officer was no more sympathetic to Maldonado than the immigration officer had been, nor was he born yesterday. And although it wasn't his job to enforce Mexican laws, it wasn't hard for him to see what Maldonado was up to and how his scheme to circumvent Mexican tariff laws had not worked. Meanwhile, Maldonado clung to his story of the car's owner being his American friend, Joe Aguirre, who would be coming to Mexico for a short vacation. He explained to the Consul that he only wanted to visit Corpus so he could give Joe back his car.

"The record shows you were in Corpus Christi last week," noted the perspicacious US Consul. Are you planning to live there, now that you have this nice American car that can't get into Mexico? Maybe you want to live with your sister who is a resident there."

"No no, nothing like that. It's not my car," Maldonado again insisted, running thorough his story once more. But his application for a visitor visa was refused on the grounds that he was likely to be an "intending immigrant." The Consul rightly felt that Maldonado did not have any pressing reason to come back into Mexico.

Maldonado adamantly refused to change his story or admit what he was trying to do, or to acknowledge that he had bought the car himself under false pretenses, although all this had become very clear to the Consul. Maldonado continued to maintain that the car belonged to his friend Joe Aguirre. Naturally the Consul considered him a likely immigrant, given that he owned a nice new car that could not enter Mexico, and that he had a sister residing in the United States, married to a US citizen. Good reason for him to want to live there too. The Consul told him he should go and apply at the US Consulate General in Monterrey, which was responsible for issuing immigrant visas for applicants from northeastern Mexico.

"But that may take weeks," he wailed.

"Sometimes a year or two," replied the experienced consular officer, sympathetically.

"But what will I do with the car?" There he was: *he* could not enter the United States, and the *car* could not enter Mexico. A rock and a hard place. "The Mexican customs people won't let me bring it into Mexico. They are keeping it in their parking lot. What should I do?"

"Well, I suggest you call Joe Aguirre in Corpus Christi and tell him to come on down and get his car. There is a public phone on the corner."

THE END

111

Short Stories Encore

Novel Material

"My wife's condition is apparently chronic; it's been treated but never completely cured," said Professor Benham, sending shivers up the spine of Mr. Lars Knutsen. "Mr. Lucky," as he was familiarly known, from his initials L.K., had been there in Huntingdon for almost a year, having come from Dayton the previous summer.

*   *   *   *   *

Most of Lucky Knutsen's career had been with a big tire company in Dayton, where he had first been a labor leader and union organizer and later the company's Employee Relations Manager. For many years Mr. Lucky, as he liked to be called, had been particularly interested in organizations and their structure. Back in his school days he studied the social structure of animal communities, ranging from social organization among tribes and clans in primitive human societies, structure of wolf packs, to species of ants and bees, and even the specialized cells in human organs, where the survival and well-being of the group has more importance than the life of any individual ant, or cell. Some modern societies view self-sacrifice of the individual for the good of the tribe or the nation as the highest form of heroism -- something to be admired and emulated, rare though it may be. However, in the USA and other Western cultures the individual is of primary importance. Self image and self esteem come first. Our children are taught to say "I am Number One" and to be proud of themselves, whether they have anything to be proud about or not. Self sacrifice is not admired. We would rather dominate other people than give up our lives for them. In fact we often view those who give up their lives for a cause as mentally deranged or irrational fanatics, even terrorists.

In his last years at the Dayton plant, Mr. Lucky wrote a book about labor organization and company organization, and the interplay of the two. Although it was written as a novel, it contained a great deal of serious substance. It went on to became a surprising best seller, and Mr. Lucky's publisher urged him to write another book about smaller social structures and the interplay of personal relationships within families and groups of individual friends.

Lucky had read and enjoyed the writings of Louis Auchincloss, and Phillip Roth, and John Barth, who sometimes set their novels in the atmosphere of a small school or college in the northeastern part of the United States. He decided that a small college town in "Main Street" America would offer rich soil in which to further study the structure and functioning of personal social relationships.

Now it so happened that Lucky's wife, Doris Knutsen, who was 15 years older than Lucky (Lucky was indifferent to age differences in couples) died just three years before Lucky was to retire from his company in Dayton. Their only daughter was by then in graduate school at UW in Madison. Lucky would put his sorrow aside and fill the void by devoting his attention to the new book and new surroundings.

For no better reason than that it wasn't too far away, and was reasonably small, and that he didn't know anybody there, Lucky decided he would set his novel in Huntingdon, Pennsylvania, the site of Juniata College.

That summer he sold his home in Dayton, put most of his furniture in storage to save for his daughter if and when she finally married, and took a furnished apartment on Allegheny Street in downtown Huntingdon. He picked up some pamphlets and brochures at the Huntingdon Chamber of Commerce and the Visitors Center, visited the Library and the Historical Society of Juniata County, ordered a newspaper subscription, and took a tour of the Juniata College campus. In short, he quietly settled in. The Huntingdon Daily News mentioned him in its Sunday social page under "New Arrivals," his modest fame as a writer and novelist having preceded him, or at least having accompanied him. Lucky was not too pleased with the publicity, for he preferred to remain in the shadows, at least in the beginning. People are often more willing to talk to a an unknown stranger than to their own brother or father. Go to any bar and look around. And listen. Lucky wanted to maintain the image of friendly stranger.

Lucky and his quiet presence were easily accepted around the little town and around the college. He attended most of the sporting events, the social events, and the cultural events that the school had to offer, and was on his way to becoming a familiar, friendly figure about town and about the Juniata campus.

One of Lucky's connections with the school came through his interest in chess. The Juniata College chess club welcomed outsiders to play against club members and even in some cases to serve as consultants or advisers to the team. It was through the chess club that Lucky met history professor Dr. Arthur Benham, adviser as well as Honorary President of the chess team. Arthur liked to talk and Lucky liked to listen -- at least he allowed himself to listen, for the good of his project. Lucky was not particularly interested in history, but he and Benham had other interests in common. They both spoke German -- Lucky's Danish grandfather spoke German, and Arthur had learned formal German en route to his Ph.D. They enjoyed good music and good wine, and Arthur liked to talk about women, especially after a drink or two. And Lucky liked to listen; he had always been open to ideas for new stories, whether they consisted of weighty and serious substance, or trivial and humorous bathos, and now he was particularly interested in material for his novel.

It soon began to appear to Lucky Knutsen that Arthur Benham liked to talk about women so much because he knew so little about them. He was married to a lively woman whom he professed to love dearly, and *did* love dearly, in his way, although they had no children.

Lucky was interested in Arthur as an example, or subject, of study. Arthur was very intelligent, wise in his academic field, a good chess player; he was well liked and had a wide range of social contacts, on and off campus. He and a few other interesting people and situations made Lucky glad he had decided to settle in a small community and college town like Huntingdon. It can be fun to look behind the scenes into what is going on in places like this.

In due course, after he had gotten to know the town and the college a little better, and had gotten to know Arthur Benham a little better, he also got to know Arthur's wife, Ingrid Benham, a little better -- as well as various other friends of the Benhams.

The Benhams had a well organized, active life: bridge once a week, tennis Saturday mornings, conferences, performing arts, faculty meetings, some with wives, some without. But much of it was a society of couples; a man could never have fitted in completely without a wife of his own, thought Lucky, but he himself, although still on the fringe, had gotten quite close to these people.

Lucky Knutsen sometimes took Arthur and Ingrid and one or two others out to dinner at "Hoss's Steak House" in downtown Huntingdon (pop 6,700), and sometimes saw them with friends at dinner parties and gatherings where an "extra man" was needed to fill an empty seat for the evening. There was one other single man on the campus who seemed close to Arthur's circles, although not of the level of Arthur's social upbringing or erudition. It was Gerhardt Auerbach, the school Athletic Director, a handsome muscle man, but an extra man nevertheless, who therefore occasionally got an invitation in some social circles merely because he was single. Juniata was proud of its academic standing, and tolerated sports like football mainly because of pressure from the alumni and because of the money athletics brought into the school coffers. Lucky once noticed a photograph of Auerbach showing off his muscles beside a picture of the football team on Arthur's desk in his study, but thought nothing of it.

Lucky was a good bit older than Arthur or Ingrid, so he was in no way viewed as a threat to their marital conjugality. Ingrid was comfortable in his presence, finding him a particularly convenient listening post, willing to hear her tell of feelings and emotions that she had to withhold from her husband's friends and colleagues who were so intimately involved with them in all their activities and school responsibilities.

It was Lucky's conscious practice, and soon a habit, to be attentive: quiet, unassuming, discrete, available. He never repeated anything he heard -- a good listener. In due course Ingrid came to rely upon Lucky when she had things on her mind. She was more comfortable with him than she was with her parish priest, and she never could have imagined herself talking to a professional counselor -- what of the social stigma if THAT had ever become known! But she could talk to Lucky when she wanted to unload on a sympathetic ear.

She told him about her husband. And about herself. In the process, in the midst of her growing friendship for Lucky, he too found, growing in himself, a feeling of gentle affection for this woman, this quiet little wife of the college professor, that was almost like love. One afternoon, when he had stopped by to lend her a book of Somerset Maugham Short Stories, she asked him to stay a minute and have a glass of wine, although it was only 3:30, not quite yet the usual cocktail hour. He stayed; no harm there. Arthur had a late class that afternoon. Ingrid was in a particularly talkative mood, no explanation as to why. Lucky held his silence and let her run on. This is what he liked -- letting someone connect with him just because he

118

was attentive and showed interest and had on a clean shirt. Little enough to give pleasure to a talker. She was enjoying letting it out. Halfway through their second glass of Chilean pinot grigio, there came out something of a surprise: "My husband doesn't do much... you know... in the bedroom anymore. We have been sleeping in separate beds since the first year we were married." Lucky held his tongue once again, tacitly replying with his gentle, understanding smile, tempered by a slight wrinkle between his eyebrows, which Ingrid seemed to find reassuring.

Then some words did come to Lucky, and still in his calm, non-threatening voice he offered, "Yes, I can understand how difficult that is. It's been almost four years since my own wife died, and I still haven't quite gotten used to living alone." What he meant, but did not say, was "not used to *sleeping* alone," but Ingrid was sensitive enough to catch the innuendo.

Indeed, Lucky had conscientiously tried not to think of women during those four years -- not think of them as romantic objects anyway. But now, with the support of a glass of wine and this friendly company, he began to reflect a little on his own feelings. He could sense that this sweet woman held -- or withheld -- strong passions within her breast. This was a Wednesday. Arthur had a late class every Wednesday. "Why don't you come again next week?" he heard her say. Indeed, why not. So he did. It became a regular thing, Wednesday afternoons. Gradually, unplanned by either of them, they began to succumb to each other's charms, and to fill a lacuna that they held in common. In due course, they did unwittingly cross the line of propriety occasionally, and it was delightful. They both agreed it was delightful -- silently, tacitly as it were -- never putting the ineffable into words.

Lucky's friendship with Arthur also continued to grow, and Arthur enjoyed having this intelligent friend who was in no way a competitor for attention or position or importance in his professional life in the college academic circles. Lucky's talent as a good listener touched Arthur almost as it had touched Ingrid. Arthur needed a friendly ear he could trust, just as had Ingrid. Arthur did not trust his social circles to silence any more than he trusted his professional colleagues, driven as they were with the competitive spirit that had already lifted them to positions of some importance in their respective fields.

Accordingly, Arthur took Lucky into his confidence to an extent Lucky found surprising, especially one evening when Ingrid was out to an SPCA meeting. Arthur had had a couple of drinks and was lamenting the increasingly dissolute state of personal morality rampant throughout the college.

He was feeling particularly garrulous for no reason at all except that, like many others, he would rather unload on this friendly stranger than on his own wife or professional colleagues. It often helps to clarify one's thoughts by putting them into spoken words.

"I could tell you a few things," he said, and then, without waiting for an answer, proceeded to do just that, suddenly sending shivers up Lucky's spine. "My wife's been having an affair."

120

Oh shit. He knows. Lucky was speechless. He didn't have anything to say, but couldn't have said it anyway. What do you say at a time like that? "Sorry, it won't happen again"? or, "We were just trying out your new couch"? or, "We didn't mean anything by it"? or, "There's nothing to worry about: we used protection"? Better just to keep the mouth shut and let him go get his six-shooter -- his Smith and Wesson .38 Special revolver -- and blast away. Justifiable homicide. Or maybe spare my life and just break both my knees if he is feeling compassionate. Lucky had never felt fear before in his life. In fact, once, some years ago, he told a friend he didn't know what fear was. Now he was beginning to find out. Now he knew.

But Benham went on. Lucky wasn't sure whether he was glad to hear what else he had to say or not. "She has been sleeping with our school doctor for several years now."

"What!" thought Lucky, momentarily stunned, with his stew of internal emotions now boiling in a new direction, "that sweet Ingrid two-timing me? I thought that outside of her husband I was the only one... and that she only loved him because she had to, because she was married to him... That's what she said," thought Lucky. "And now I'm a cuckold!"

Lucky wasn't able to say anything, fortunately. There was nothing for him to say that could have helped things. He looked at Arthur, and a feeling of brotherly sympathy shot through him. "Poor fellow, I know just how you feel," he thought, with his heart going out to him. "He's in the same boat I'm in. He's a cuckold too!"

121

But Arthur ignored Lucky's silence and went on, talking about the doctor. "Apparently Dr. Philpot has unlimited supplies of Salvarsan and 606 and stuff like that as well as penicillin of course. So he has been able to ward off any serious effects and hold the infection at bay."

Serious effects? Infection? Salvarsan? 606? What's he talking about?

"Salvarsan?" Lucky muttered.

"Yes, Salvarsan. Ingrid has syphilis. She caught it at a tender age, and now it's chronic. Although she likes to pretend it was congenital, I was never sure. True, it's been controlled, but it has never been completely cured or eradicated. She is still carrying mild traces of it. I love her dearly, but our love of course is not the same as usual love between a husband and wife, especially in a physical sense. We haven't been in the same bed together since the first year of our marriage, but we still sleep right in the same room and have our twin beds near each other. So we are still really very close."

"How nice," thought Lucky sarcastically, although he already knew about that arrangement.

Still Benham went on: "Doctor Philpot has unlimited supplies of prophylactic medication that he gave me and that he must also douse himself with, so I don't think he has ever caught it. But he says she is still contagious and always will be."

"Contagious? Yuck!" thought Lucky, as he began to scratch an imaginary itch. "I wonder whether he suspects me and is trying to scare me to keep me at bay. Maybe he is saying that just to keep Ingrid for himself. Maybe Doctor Philpot's wife -- her name is Angeline -- has been playing with the athletic director or somebody, and the good doctor had to find someone else to play with, just to get even. I should investigate that possibility," he thought, "it might be good material for another story."

Lucky's thoughts raced on: "Maybe I'd better go see Dr. Philpot myself, he seems so experienced. I'll stop by another day and give poor Ingrid a kiss on the cheek. She really is a very sweet woman."

But before he could break away, Arthur let him know he still had something to say. The whisky had gone to his head, perhaps, and after all this he still wasn't through. "But I love her. I really do," Arthur insisted. "I don't mind being tolerant toward her peccadilloes with the good doctor. I think I would rather it be he than anybody else I know. I don't know what will happen when Philpot dies," he said with a benign glance at Lucky, or did he imagine it?

Lucky's sympathy for Arthur was now equaled by pity and concern for himself, as he scratched himself once more in silence.

"You know," Arthur went on, "she really is very sweet and tolerant. She doesn't get upset when I see Gerhardt sometimes."

That was when Lucky remembered the photograph of the muscle man on Arthur's desk, in the tight T-shirt with the shoulders cut out showing off his well-developed deltoids.

Small town, thought Lucky. I could write a book about it.

THE END

Kill or Be Killed

"Kill or be killed," bellowed the Sergeant. "It's as simple as that. You need to forget any sweet ideas or ideals you ever had for sympathy or compassion. The only good enemy is a dead enemy, and if you die you are no good anymore to your unit or the US Army, or the United States of America or your girlfriend or anybody else. No good! You got that? We don't need any pacifists or C.O.'s out here, and if you start feeling sorry for the enemy, we'll start feeling sorry for you, posthumously, because you will be dead. It's them or us and it's him or you. You gotta use your brains and not take any unnecessary risks. And do as you are told. You got that? Well, git it!" That was the sergeant talking to all of us, the whole platoon. Then later on he got me alone and lit into me:

"And you listen here, Private Jasper. You get rid of that book, because if I catch you reading it again I'll put you on report for aiding and betting on the enemy."

"Reading a book is not aiding and abetting the enemy, Sir," I meekly contended. "You can't tell anybody, even a soldier, what to read or what not to read in his off-duty hours."

"You have to kill or be killed," he roared sardonically. "It's a matter of life and death. How many times do I have to tell you that?

125

"But Sir..."

"I'm telling you, don't read that trash."

"I can read anything I want to."

"Yes, but not that."

"You can't stop me."

"We'll see about that."

The book in question was the famous war story by Eric Maria Remarque about World War I, *All Quiet on the Western Front.* It was written soon after the end of that war, known then as "The Great War." Its title in German was *Im Westen Nichts Neues,* and it won its author a Nobel Prize. I got it from my older sister, who is a peace-marching pacifist. She stuck it into my bag as I was heading off to boot camp, and I hadn't had a chance to read it until now. I have to agree with the Sergeant that she probably shouldn't have done it, but I didn't feel he had the right to dictate what I was allowed to read.

The book is of course intensely anti-war, and depicts gruesome images of death and suffering on the front lines during WWI. But wars are different today. There used to be point-blank shooting from one side to the other, and even hand-to-hand combat, which is rare now. Although we still use grenades and mortars, we also have new and more effective ways of killing. We have artillery fire and rocket fire directed by GPS, position-directed aerial bombing, and, more recently, the drones, pilot-less aircraft

126

that can take out a target by remote control, killing lots of the enemy without risking the death of an American pilot. Drones give us very favorable kill ratios, but they do cause a few collateral deaths and are frightfully expensive.

The picture of war given in the Remarque book is different from the wars we are fighting today. However, it does make its point of giving a vivid picture of the horror, and futility, of all wars. Not good morale-building material for a combat soldier. Well, I hadn't wanted to be a combat soldier anyway. I had been drafted. I looked forward to getting out when my time was up, and then going to peace marches with my sister at the first opportunity.

But right now I had to defend my right to freedom of the press or freedom of speech or whatever. I had to stand up against this combat-hardened sergeant, whose looks alone made my knees tremble.

"All right, Sir, then we'll take it to the Colonel," I said, pretending I was Jimmy Stewart in a John Wayne movie. "He said he was always open to problems or questions."

Sarge wasn't too pleased, but we did it. We went to the Colonel, and the Sergeant started in:

"Sir, this man has been wasting time reading an improper book he has no business even having here in a combat zone. I think he should get rid of it, Sir."

The Colonel naturally asked, "What book are you talking about?" but he was looking at me.

I felt a surge of adrenalin, knowing I was within my rights, so I spoke up rather boldly, "You mean you have to know, Sir? Does that mean you might approve of some books but would censor others? Is that why you have to know?

"Are you getting smart with me?"

"Sir?"

"I said I don't like smart-Alecs"

"Yes Sir."

"Well"

"It's a book about war, Sir."

"That sounds all right. What's its name?"

"*Im Westen Nichts Neues*, Sir."

"What?"

"*Im Westen Nichts Neues*. It means 'Nothing New in the West.' It won its author a Nobel prize. Some people call it *All Quiet on the Western Front*."

"What's it about -- cowboys and Indians killing each other?"

"Yes Sir, something like that. Killing anyway. You've got the idea."

"I never would have thought a Western like that could win a Noble Prize. That stuff is mostly trash."

"Oh, I liked *The Riders of the Purple Sage* too; we even read it in school.

"Yes, I think I've heard of that one."

"But this one is even better than Zane Gray," I said. "A lot of people get killed, both Good Guys and Bad Guys. You might like it, Sir. Maybe you ought to read it."

"I doubt it," said the Colonel. "Sergeant, I agree with you that it's sad this man wants to read such Western junk, but I don't see any pressing reason to keep him from doing it."

"But Sir..."

"That's all, Sergeant."

*   *   *   *   *

So I won. But it was a Pyrrhic victory. I won the case but lost the battle. I never should have confronted the Sergeant with my judicious claims of right to free speech and free choice of reading material. The next two months were wretched for me. The frumious Sergeant made sure of that. He also made sure he did nothing to me that was outside of Army regulations or the Code of Military Justice. But he was still able to make my life miserable, all in the name of toughening up his troops and keeping them combat ready. Extra exercises, extra inspections, extra practice in

129

disassembling and reassembling my rifle, our mortars, our recoil-less rifles. Extra practice in memorizing and reciting our rules for combat and combat procedures as contained in our infantry field manuals.

We were required to be familiar with our FM's, or Field Manuals; in my case that meant having to memorize them. I memorized all the ways I could kill the enemy, or be killed myself if I didn't watch out. From time to time, when other soldiers in my battalion or even my regiment were killed, I could tell you in which manual and on what page that type of casualty was described, and the preventive measures or evasive action that should have been taken, but wasn't. "Never expose your head," the manual advised. What should we do, leave our head back at camp when we went off on patrol? You can laugh if you want to, but it wasn't funny out there in those desert towns.

Our job from time to time was to "clear and hold" one village or another. There was never much secrecy in what we did; in fact the opposite was usually the case. With all the hoopla and adverse publicity about collateral deaths and the killing of civilians, we started announcing our intentions to clear this village or that village a few days ahead of time, dropping leaflets and sending out radio broadcasts telling all civilians or non-combatants to evacuate the area before such and such a date.

Then the bombardment would begin. At first it was conventional aerial attacks with ordinary little 500-pound bombs, but sometimes with drones, artillery barrages if we were lucky enough to have a support battery available, our own self-propelled 75-mm canons, and finally mere mortars, flame-throwers, grenades, and recoil-less rocket rifles that we carried ourselves.

Sometimes by the time we entered a village "on foot," which usually meant riding in armored personnel carriers, or APC's, all we found was smoking ruins, perhaps with an occasional roof-top sharpshooter who had been left behind to give up his life while taking a few other lives with him. Such sharpshooters usually helped to give the enemy a good kill ratio, sometimes four- or five-to-one, or even ten-to-one better than ours. We always got such sharpshooters in the end though. Almost always.

Our job was to cull through the ruins and any buildings left standing to ensure that the enemy had completely withdrawn or had already been killed. It was gruesome work, sometimes made even more unpleasant when we found pathetic townsfolk huddled in a basement or a church who had sick or frightened children, or old parents, or other excuses as to why they could not evacuate. We constantly regretted collateral casualties and broken families.

On one of our village-clearing operations, our supporting artillery battery lost communications with us. It seems the problem was caused either by electronic disturbance in the ionosphere or by the malfunctioning of one of our own radio-jamming devices used to disrupt the enemy's communications. At any rate, the artillery barrage was resumed long after it was supposed to have ceased fire. My patrol had already entered the village, and suddenly our friendly fire forced us to scatter for protective cover, wherever we could find it.

131

I jumped into the basement entryway of a demolished building, several feet below the level of the street. When the bullets and shell fragments are flying, you want to get *down.* That's the first thing they tell you in boot camp and in your infantry manual. Good advice.

It was late afternoon, and it was dark in there. Then I saw something move. At first I didn't realize that the stairwell had another occupant. Another man. Another soldier. As I started to speak I noticed he looked strange. Strange outfit. Not one of ours. Enemy uniform. The enemy.

This realization came faster than it takes to tell of it. Intense training had honed my reflexes to a keen sensitivity. The enemy. You act fast, instinctively, without a second thought. I bayoneted him, straight in the middle. It was just like practice in training where you jab the dummies stuffed with cotton and styrofoam. The only difference was that it was harder to pull my bayonet out this time; it had gotten stuck on a recalcitrant rib or something tough inside the man. Later, the picture I carried in my mind was like that of high school football practice, where we charged a padded iron sledge that was our foe.

Modern soldiers rarely use their bayonets; often they do not even carry them anymore. We patrolled with fixed bayonets mostly for the image they gave us of aggressive no-nonsense troops bent on thorough clearing of the village. Lucky for me.

"Ah," said the soldier as I pulled my rifle back and got the bayonet out of his chest. Or maybe he said, "Ouch," or "Ow!" I'm not sure.

132

I suddenly realized what I had done. I looked at him closely for the first time. The light was dim, but I could see that he was young, probably not more than nineteen, pale skin, no beard that I could see. The age of my own brother. The most horrible moment of my life. Have I killed him? Will he die? I have never killed a man before. Only now did I begin to think... to have thoughts.

Then he spoke again, or tried to. Blood was pouring from his mouth and it was clearly with great difficulty that he said, "Wa... " Water, of course. He wants water.

I turned to get my canteen and was unscrewing the top when the pistol shots rang out.

I felt something like a bee sting on the side of my neck, and a powerful slap on the shoulder that almost knocked me over. Then I must have fainted, for that's all I remember.

THE END

Epilogue

I was evacuated, spent a while in hospital, ultimately got discharged both from the hospital and from the Army, and got a purple heart and a copper star for meritorious service -- for killing an enemy soldier. It turned out he was an eighteen-year-old lieutenant. I was lucky to be alive; enemy officers sometimes carry pistols, they explained.

Yes, I knew that.

THE SECOND END

P.S.

Along with my medals, the Adjutant General's Office also said that, because of my bravery and heroism, they were bending Army regulations somewhat and were presenting me with a prize of war. The pistol.

That, I declined.

THE FINAL END

Believing

It is amazing what some people believe.

It is also amazing what some people say they believe.

And furthermore, it is amazing what some people *do*, after telling us what they believe.

I am thinking about people and religion. Religion is a strange thing. Where did it come from? If it came from God or Gods, where did God or Gods come from?

All right, so there are unanswered questions that mankind (and of course womankind) have pondered over, throughout the millennia. Questions that have always been with us. How we answer them, or try to answer them, is very different among different groups of people or areas, and in different epochs of human history and development.

Much of the origins of religion must have grown out of the ignorance of primitive peoples, and their efforts to find or imagine some sort of explanation for various events and aspects of nature that they did not understand. It wasn't always so simple as attributing the cause of thunder to the noise of wagons or chariots rolling about above the clouds, but was often more complicated than that. Something, or someone, must be the cause of the rising and setting of the sun and the moon. Something or someone must have put the stars where they are, caused the ocean tides, made the

135

rain drops fall, created the wind and river currents, built the mountains, planted the first forests, designed the flowers and animals.

All these things and events that people saw had to have some cause. There had to be something behind it all, and people called it God or Gods. Man needed some sort of explanation or rationale in his own mind for the phenomena he saw about him.

Religion offered explanations for a lot of things. It explained causes and also explained purposes. It helped explain "why" in both senses of that word, namely "from what cause?" and "for what purpose?" Religion offers answers to both these questions.

Another important aspect of religion is that it helped to perpetuate the race, or at least propagate its own devotees or tribes. Just as people and societies have gotten more complicated over time, so religions have too. Perhaps, a long time ago, a part (or maybe even most) of man's thoughts derived from his religion. Nowadays it is possible to choose a religion that seems best to fit with the beliefs one already has, rather than the other way around.

One can even choose to have no religion at all. It was hard to do that thousands of years ago, when people needed the idea of rumbling chariots above the clouds to explain thunder.

And then some practical people, or pragmatic and materialistic people, came along who said we didn't need a God or Gods to explain things we didn't understand. It was the discharge of static electricity among the clouds or between a cloud and the ground that caused thunder and lightning. And there were also reasons, besides the Gods, real reasons, that trees grew in the forest, even if we did not understand them all -- how chlorophyll converted the energy of the sun into starch and plant life, how capillary action explained the miraculous rise and fall of life-giving xylem and phloem juices in the bark of a tree.

But for most people it was comforting to know that there were Godly forces behind their lives and the happenings in this world, and that, for the most part, if we did the right thing -- if we did what God (or the Gods) wanted us to do -- we would be all right. Then the Gods would be happy and might even take care of us. These ideas were then written down in places like the Torah, the Bible, and the Qur'an. And even on our belt buckles and our money, where we like to spell it out and reassure ourselves that God is with us.

However, as people learned more about the real world around them, some of them began to realize that not all unusual events had to have a religious or supernatural cause.

Thomas Jefferson was one of those who were skeptical about the need for such supernatural events and explanations as are found in the Holy Bible. He thereupon prepared his own version of the Bible, one having no accounts of anything supernatural. Apparently what was merely natural was adequate and complicated enough for Jefferson. And so he produced "The Jefferson Bible," essentially the King James without the miracles.

137

Other people have questioned the need to rely upon unsubstantiated beliefs.   However, in some religions, holding to a belief without substantial grounds for doing so is considered particularly holy and admirable: one who can believe without having seen is more blessèd than one who believes *because* he has seen.   People who are truly devout will tell you that the essence of their religion must be faith, faith being acceptance and belief of things that cannot be seen or proven.   Because there are many things that cannot be seen or proven, faith may go a long way and can be a powerful sustaining force for believers.

But some people may still be skeptical.   Take my brother for instance.   He is a good guy, very bright, very knowledgeable, very compassionate, concerned for the health and well-being of peoples everywhere, but he is something of a skeptic when it comes to religion.   Only half jokingly, he gives his definition of faith: "Faith is believing what you know ain't so."   Maybe he would like the Jefferson Bible; I should get him one.

There are a lot of other people who profess certain religious beliefs but who in their actions do not support what they say they believe.   I have noticed this in others over the years, and have even begun to notice it in myself. I was doing things I didn't believe in, or believing in things I wasn't doing.

I sat down and started to try to understand my problem. I wrote little notes and bits and pieces about what I was supposed to believe, and what I was able to believe, and what I was supposed to do. These notes seemed to evolve into some sort of a sermon -- a sermon to myself, but perhaps a sermon for other people as well.

I wondered whether my church would let me give my little sermon from the pulpit some Sunday. Here it is. You can tell me what you think of it. It was intended to be sarcastic and humorous as well as indicative of my present confusion regarding some of these religious matters.

*　*　*　*　*

WHY I AM NOT A CHRISTIAN

I am not a Christian because I do not follow the teachings of Jesus Christ, and in fact I do not believe in many of them.

The teachings of Christ were summarized for us in the Gospel of St. Matthew, that portion known as the "Sermon on the Mount." Let's have a look:

The Teachings of Christ: Saint Matthew, Chapter 5:

5-21 *et seq*. Thou shalt not kill; furthermore do not harbour anger toward your brother, and make peace with your brother before you bring offerings to God.

5-25 Agree with thine adversary quickly; that is, if someone brings a lawsuit against you, settle the dispute while there is time, before you get to court.

5-32 If a man divorces his wife for any cause other than her unfaithfulness, then he is guilty of making her commit adultery if she marries again, and the man who marries her commits adultery also.

5-36 Do not swear... Just say "Yes" or "No" -- anything else you say comes from the Evil One.

5-39 Resist not evil, but whosoever shall smite thee on thy right cheek, turn to him the other also. And if someone takes you to court to sue you for your shirt, let him have your coat as well.

5-44 Love your enemies, bless them that curse you, do good to them that hate you, and pray for them who spitefully use you and persecute you.

6-1 Take heed that you do not do your alms before men. Make certain that you do not perform your religious duties in public so that people will see what you do.

6-5 When you do pray, do not be like the hypocrites. They love to stand up and pray in the houses of worship and on the street corners, so that everyone will see them.

6-7 When ye pray, do not use vain repetitions, as the heathen do, for they think they shall be heard for their much speaking.

6-14 If ye forgive men their trespasses, that is, if you forgive others the wrongs they have done to you, your Father in heaven will also forgive you. But if ye forgive not men their trespasses, neither will your Father forgive your trespasses.

6-19 Lay not up for yourselves treasures upon earth, where moth and rust doth corrupt and where thieves break through and steal.

6-25 Do not be worried about the food and drink you need in order to stay alive, or about clothes for your body.

7-1 Judge not, that ye be not judged. With what judgement ye judge, ye shall be judged. First take the log out of your own eye, and then you will be able to see clearly to take the speck out of your brother's eye.

7-12 All things whatsoever ye would that men should do to you, do ye even so to them.

* * * * *

Now let's consider each of these teachings:

5-21 Thou shalt not kill; furthermore do not harbor anger toward your brother and make peace with your brother before you bring offerings to God.

I cannot accept that. Not kill? I keep a gun in my bedroom drawer, and if an intruder were to threaten me or my family, I would blast away at him. I am proud to know that American troops are killing all the militants they can find in Iraq as well as any terrorists or suspected terrorists in Iraq or Afghanistan or any other place where they may be found. I know that my tax dollars are going to pay for the airplanes and bombs and tanks and drones and other military expenses that are necessary for the defense and security of our great nation. Sure we have the death

141

penalty in Texas. Murderers should be put away for good. Somebody should tell *them* thou shalt not kill. My own daughter was murdered. You want me to harbor no anger toward her killer? (even though he is now dead too). I bring my offerings to God, but don't ask me to make peace with my daughter's murderer or Saddam Hussein or Osama bin Laden, even if you think they are my brothers. So I am not following Christ on this one.

5-25 Agree with thine adversary quickly;   that is, if someone brings a lawsuit against you, settle the dispute while there is time, before you get to court.

I think the purpose of our courts is to ensure that the laws are proper and that they are upheld, and if I have a case I have every right to take it to court and get everything that the law allows. I once mentioned to a lawyer friend that I had read Japan has far fewer lawyers than the United States, and in fact we have 100 times more lawyers than they do, on a per capita basis, in proportion. The lawyer smartly replied, "Yes, we are a nation of laws." And I say, if you have a case, take it to court. I don't follow Christ on this.

5-32 If a man divorces his wife for any cause other than her unfaithfulness, then he is guilty of making her commit adultery if she marries again, and the man who marries her commits adultery also.

I have been divorced twice, and I don't think the cause was unfaithfulness in either case. So I haven't followed Christ here.

5-36 Do not swear... Just say "Yes" or "No" -- anything else you say comes from the Evil One.

I swear, and not just cussing. I swear allegiance to the Flag, and to the Country for which it stands. I swore when I went into the military and again when I went into government service as a civilian. The time I went to court in Texas I think swore on a bible that I would tell the truth, the same King James Bible that tells me I should just say yes or no, but not swear. So I haven't followed Christ's teachings here either.

And I swear (to tell the truth) once a month when I serve as Spanish interpreter at the Jasper County Municipal Court. And I remember the Acadians, who were exiled in 1763 because they would only "avow" but, for religious reasons, would not "swear" allegiance to George III and England.

5-39 Resist not evil, but whosoever shall smite thee on thy right cheek, turn to him the other also. And if someone takes you to court to sue you for your shirt, let him have your coat as well.

Resist not evil? What will *that* ever get us? Hit me on my right cheek and I'll paste you a good one on *your* right cheek, or left cheek, or maybe both. If someone takes me to court, I will try to get everything out of him that is my due. Is Christ saying we should not resist terrorists like the ones responsible for 9/11? Maybe He just doesn't realize what a terrible threat those evil people are to us. I can't use Christ's teachings here. Sorry.

143

5-44 Love your enemies, bless them that curse you, do good to them that hate you, and pray for them who spitefully use you and persecute you.

Come on! Did you expect me to love Hitler and Osama bin Laden and all those other SOB's that hate *us*? My first wife hated me for trying to continue to be a part of our children's lives after the divorce. Hated me. Was I supposed to love her for that? I'm afraid I can't love my enemies and others that hate *me*. Sorry, Jesus.

6-1 Take heed that you do not do your alms before men. Make certain that you do not perform your religious duties in public so that people will see what you do.

When I and my friends contribute a little to the local Hospice, or even to the Arts Council or the Conservation League, or to our high school or college development fund, we love to look through the quarterly list of donors to ensure our name is spelled correctly, (and see who else is there!) And what an added delight to see a star by our names showing everyone that we have contributed for five years straight! But not exactly in accordance with Christ's teaching. (Even our top Christian preparatory schools list your name with a star if you have been a consistent donor.)

6-5 When you do pray, do not be like the hypocrites! They love to stand up and pray in the houses of worship and on the street corners, so that everyone will see them.

When I go to church I like to sing in the choir, up front, where people can see me. After church, friends and acquaintances greet me and tell me the choir was great, even if in truth it was only mediocre. I like to see who is in church, and I must confess I like for others to see me there too, even if Christ says I shouldn't be that way.

6-7   When ye pray, do not use vain repetitions, as the heathen do, for they think they shall be heard for their much speaking.

I love it when we sing Haendel's Messiah, especially the part that goes Hallelujah, Hallelujah, Hallelujah. There is quite a bit of repetition in our other prayers too. Sometimes they are almost like a chant, and that way they can be very moving, very emotional. Why does He tell us not to use vain repetitions? We like our repetitions. Every week we repeat the same prayers.

6-14   If ye forgive men their trespasses, that is if you forgive others the wrongs they have done to you, your Father in heaven will also forgive you. But if ye forgive not men their trespasses, neither will your Father forgive your trespasses.

Forgiveness sounds good in principle, but how can I forgive the 9/11 terrorists for crashing into the Twin Towers and killing over two thousand people? It is all I can do to forgive the North Vietnamese, but should I forgive Castro too, for setting up his oppressive regime ninety miles offshore from the United States? And I don't think I will ever be able to forgive my wife who got the best divorce lawyer in Boston and practically cleaned me out financially, using every legal loophole, and some that weren't even legal (as I learned later).

145

6-19 Lay not up for yourselves treasures upon earth, where moth and rust doth corrupt and where thieves break through and steal.

I have to confess that I do hold on to a few material things and what little bit of wealth I do have. I have a small government pension, and I own a house and have a little money in the bank and a couple of shares on the New York Stock Exchange. It's not a lot, and I must confess that I wouldn't mind if it were more, and if my shares go up in value next Monday, I won't mind that either. I have a materialistic consideration in my life that is too deeply set for me to take to heart the admonition not to lay up treasures. The truth is I would if I could. We call it Yankee thrift. I just never had much opportunity to do so.

6-25 Do not be worried about the food and drink you need in order to stay alive, or about clothes for your body.

Well, like most thinking people I know, I have health insurance as well as life insurance, and I have even consulted a financial adviser with regard to my financial requirements after retirement. Should I not worry about where my food and drink are coming from? Sounds like the comic character, "What, me worry?" I have to fail this one.

7-1 Judge not, that ye be not judged. With what judgement ye judge, ye shall be judged. First take the log out of your own eye, and then you will be able to see clearly to take the speck out of your brother's eye.

Here I am, look at me, implicitly judging my church-going friends and others who profess to call themselves Christians, but who in fact may not be much nearer to being Christian than I am. I fail this one too; I am judging other people almost every day. I have been taught to use judgement before I choose my friends and business associates.

7-12 All things whatsoever ye would that men should do to you, do ye even so to them.

Ah yes, the Golden Rule. I think this is fundamental, or at least accepted, by all religions in the world that I have ever heard of. Perhaps it is the essence of being a Godly person. But how can I practice it? Should I help a stranger fix a flat by the roadside? My clothes are cleaner than his and I might get them dirty. Or he might bash my head in with his tire iron and take my money. Would I take advantage of a business deal where I would not have liked to be the other person? Probably. After all, business is business.

* * * * *

On looking over these pages and reflecting on what I have written, I have to conclude that it looks as though being a Christian would really be tough, and I fear that I just don't have what it takes. Also, as I look around me... but then, alas, one of the things I am not supposed to do is judge others.

My name is Daniel, which comes from Hebrew and means "May God be my judge." But I would not stand up well under His judgement.

I pray for greater strength; I pray that I might be a better person.

And I pray for forgiveness.

I pray that Christ will forgive me for not being a Christian.

In the name of Christ.

Amen.

END OF PROPOSED TEXT

I asked my minister for permission to speak to the congregation some day. He wanted to read the text of what I planned to say, so I gave it to him, thinking he might actually be impressed by the depth of my thoughts, and the extent of my research, and the keenness of my insights.

But it didn't work. His reply was, "No, I don't think it would be such a good idea right now."

THE END
Epilogue

Maybe I should go find another religion where they would accept it. I have heard that there still exist obscure religious sects where you don't have to be Christian to get in, and where you can always speak your thoughts, sarcastic though they may appear.

THE FINAL END

Oh, Woe Is Me

My husband, Eugene, is a rather rough and tough sort of fellow. Well, tough anyway. However, I do love him; sometimes he can be a bit tender, even sweet. But he never did like his name much; he thought it sounded weak and sissy. He was afraid it would remind people of Eugene O'Neill, who, my husband learned, was either gay or a borderline case as attested by his numerous gay friends and acquaintances (although that was before the euphemistic term "gay" came into the lexicon). So maybe my Eugene overcompensated a bit. He liked to work out regularly, pump iron, and exercise on the machines at the gym to build up his muscles. And that was all right with me. I like a man who is in good physical shape, and I keep myself in good physical shape too. When a husband and wife are both in good physical shape it adds to their pleasure of doing things together. But we both wanted to postpone starting a family. It was something we thought about and of course something I worried about when I was with Eugene because I wasn't ready to start having babies yet.

Eugene was a policeman before I knew him, then a security guard for a private company. After I married him he became Executive Director for the whole security operation. One of the things his time as a security guard taught him was the important work that could be done by well-trained dogs working with security personnel. He was so fascinated by the strength of powerful guard dogs that, even after he became an executive in his company, he kept

149

several dogs of his own, and enjoyed training them to be as strong and vicious as possible. Although dog-fighting was illegal in our area, and possibly in the rest of the nation as well, South Carolina had some remote counties where dog-fighting was popular as a spectator sport and for gambling. It was even more popular than cock-fighting, which was declared illegal in the 1960's. Back then there was one little company that had done nothing but raise cocks for cockfighting, under the motto, "Our cocks don't f... around." /1 They made quite a lot of money.

Eugene decided he could significantly add to his salary by training dogs for "The Pits," the name given to the dog-fighting ring, or arena. As we lived out in the country, about ten miles from town, Eugene built kennels and a "training field," and bought and started training a dozen or more puppies of the best fighting breeds he could think of, mostly pit bulls, rottweilers, doberman pinchers, and a few German police dogs. The puppies were awfully cute and playful, I must say, and I thought it a shame that he had to teach them to be fighters.

"I am only helping to bring out their natural instincts," he insisted. "I am just giving them a chance to fulfill the potential that their genes and nature have given them.".

/1 Some years later, when the Fighting Gamecocks were the mascots of the University of South Carolina, some enterprising students demonstrated their wit and academic allegiance by printing up and selling at cost 10,000 T-shirts boldly reading, "You Can't Lick Our Cocks." I understand that they are now heirlooms bringing a free-market price of $125 to $200 each.

When the dogs were old enough to begin fighting, they began fighting. Eugene would take two or three with him in the pick-up truck over to the next county where the "pits" were. That went on for a couple of years. His dogs were not doing particularly well, only about average. They won some and lost some. Some were torn up a bit and had to have veterinarian attention, and one or two of them even died or had to be euthanized. But Eugene did not give up. He kept working on his dog-training methods, reading everything he could on the subject, including reports of fighting techniques between other species of animals. He was particularly intrigued by a short film he saw of fights among alpacas, or llamas, in Peru. These animals, poorly known to most of the industrialized world, fought naturally and viciously, without even having been trained to do so. Eugene was fascinated to see that their most effective fighting technique was to go for the testicles of the adversary. Almost invariably the animal who first bit off the balls of his opponent was the winner. It is hard to keep up your fighting spirit when another dog is chewing on your testicles or if you have no balls at all. It must be excruciating and is probably very painful too. But the technique seemed promising, perhaps even worth developing.

"I'll bet I could teach some of my dogs to do that," thought Eugene. So that's what he decided to do. He bought some pigs for targets, because he didn't want to hurt any of his good dogs too much in this training process. He might need them later for stud service if they kept up their good health and good records among the dog-fighting community.

151

Eugene thereupon cooked up some beef bouillon flavored with Teriyaki sauce which he showed to his dogs and then dabbed on to the appropriate after extremities of the pig. He turned both the pig and the dog loose, with instructions to the dog to "Go sic 'em." Well, let me tell you, that dog didn't need to be told twice or thrice. Indeed, in just a trice, before the pig was halfway across the training field, the dog had his nose right in there where it was supposed to go, and his teeth and jaws were there too. Eugene knew right away that his experiment was a success when the pig let out the most Gawd-awful squeal and screech and scream he had ever heard, while it was running at full speed with this most unpleasant and unimaginably painful piece of baggage clamped on behind her. I mean him. (Later, Eugene did think of training female dogs, called bitches, to be fighters, because he figured their lesser vulnerability in this regard would give them a certain advantage, but he dropped that idea because the bitches were not quite so aggressive as the males.)

Now the interesting thing is that when he repeated the experiment Eugene found that the bouillon soup flavored with Teriyaki sauce was not necessary; that the dogs seemed to know right where to go, upon merely being told to "go get his balls." It seems that this fighting instinct was innate in the primordial genes of certain canine animals. Perhaps it is the reason the species survived after the demise of its adversaries eons ago. Survival of the fittest, some have called it. Might makes right. To the victor go the spoils. Hit 'em where it hurts. Don't shoot until you see the whites of their eye...balls.

152

Eugene then told his fighting dogs to put this new battle strategy into practice. Back at the dog-fighting pit, all he had to do was whisper into his dog's ear, "Go get his balls." It worked every time. Eugene won every bet and lost some of his friends -- friends who were unwise enough to dare set their dogs up in opposition to Eugene's dogs and bet on them. It was the easiest money Eugene had ever made. All he was doing was using the right breed and relying upon the breed's deeply ingrained, age-old instincts.

Eugene was the happiest of men, with a job he still liked, and an avocation he liked, and a wife he liked... me... who still loved him and loved to be with him, especially in the evening when he wasn't out with his dogs.

Yes, I still loved him... I am sure I did... although I was never very comfortable being related, even by marriage, to what I thought was a rather horrible operation involving all this dog-fighting. I don't even like the idea of gambling. I have seen people who lost what they could not afford to lose. Maybe for some compulsive gamblers the thrill comes precisely from the fact that they cannot afford to lose what they are losing. If they could afford to lose, it wouldn't be so thrilling -- not such an exciting gamble.

Well, as I was saying, all this went on for a number of years, although I was never comfortable with what my husband was doing with the dogs and dog-fighting.

Then something happened.

Eugene rarely let any of the dogs come into the house, but one Saturday afternoon he did just that. He let in

Bruno, one of his favorite pit bulls, and spent most of the afternoon in his favorite chair watching the Clemson-Georgia Tech football game while scratching the dog's ear by his side. We were planning to go out to dinner, so when the game ended he went into the bathroom to take a shower, and, I suppose, to get the doggie smell off his hands. He should have put the dog outside right then, but he didn't.

After his shower, with just a towel loosely wrapped around him, he opened the bathroom door to head for the bedroom and get dressed. The dog heard the door open and was there to meet him in the hallway. Apparently the esurient beast saw something enticing hanging there arousing his keenly honed primordial instincts, whereupon he quickly leaped up and voraciously bit off his master's thumb.

Eugene let out a scream that the EMS people could have heard three miles away, but I called 911 anyway, surmising that he might have been hurt. Then, as I saw blood everywhere, my suspicions were confirmed. I was quite sure something had happened, possibly serious.

I quickly threw a bathrobe around Eugene, who was still making unusually loud noises and thrashing about, apparently in considerable discomfort, and got him to the front door just as the ambulance was coming up the drive. There was of course a lot of blood on the floor and all around. I also saw there on the floor by the bathroom door what looked like a piece of meat; oh, my God, it looks like a human thumb! It must be my husband's thumb; it couldn't be anybody else's. That naughty doggie bit off my husband's thumb in his excitement! Good that he didn't eat it. I'll take it along to the hospital; maybe they can sew it back on. I have heard of remarkable things like that. I wrapped the slimy, bloody thing in my handkerchief.

Eugene didn't stop screaming and hollering all the way to the hospital, so I knew there was something definitely hurting him as he is usually quite sanguine and forbearing, even in times of discomfort and distress.

Because of all the blood everywhere, as soon as we got to the hospital they rushed him into the first operating room available and began to do what they could to help stop the blood. I grabbed one of the interns standing by and gave him my folded handkerchief containing my dear husband's thumb. "Perhaps you can sew it back on," I said.

"Good thinking," he replied with a mild smile, unfolding the cloth. However he then added, "but I don't think this is a thumb. In fact, it looks rather more like a... like a... "

"Yes? Like a... ?"

"Well, like a testicle."

"Oh me! Oh my Goodness! Well then, you *must* sew it back on. Please, you *absolutely* have to sew it back on! Whatever it costs!"

"Of course, we will do what we can," said the intern, who wasn't even the surgeon, but was proud of his college education. "Now you just be calm; I am sure everything will be all right. Many men have lived successful and productive lives and without a testicle or two, especially in the olden days. Some of them even developed their condition into a profession and a career, working in the seraglios and singing in the concert halls."

"Oh dear! But what about me? What is going to become of me? I'll be married to a man who is a... what's the word... ? It's a Greek word I think. It begins with eu. The Greeks had those kinds of men, and maybe the Romans too. They used them to guard the doors to the Harems because they didn't have to worry about them with the ladies. They were *eunuchs* -- that's it. But I always worry when my husband is with me -- close to me. I don't want to be married to a man I don't have to worry about!

"Oh, woe is me!"

THE END

Fifty Cents

I am an old man now, and I have done everything -- well almost everything -- that I ever really wanted to do in this life, including some things I was supposed to do, plus a few things I wasn't supposed to do. Now I am tired. My joints ache. Even the parts of me that are between my joints -- or join my joints -- ache. My organs are also slowing down -- most of them. All of me is wearing out, and I am virtually a walking "One Hoss Shay," as Oliver Wendell Holmes would have said, and as was explained in an earlier story of this series. /1

I know I won't live much longer, and that is all right with me. I have written my will, made my funeral arrangements, fed the dog, changed my socks and put on clean underwear, and instead of Christmas cards I have sent out some postal cards to close family members and relatives plus a few friends that I probably won't see anymore. Postal cards are the ones you buy at the post office, with the stamps already printed on them, not like postcards, which need a stamp, and require a certain amount of effort in tearing the sticky little things out of a booklet or off a roll and licking them or peeling the backs off them and sticking them somewhere near the corner of your card or envelope. Your postal cards can also serve as Christmas cards -- all you have to do is write "Merry

/1 See "Oh, All Right," SHORT STORIES FOREVER, p 153.

Christmas" or "Happy Hanukkah" on them. It is possible that some of these people may see me again, especially if the funeral home lays me out in a half-open coffin for a couple of days and gives out public notice. But my friends are getting old too, and even if they come to see me, by then many of them may be too old to be recognizable.

I have one particular friend who runs a little restaurant not far from where I live. The food is good and the prices are right, so I eat there quite often. He specializes in seafood, and it just so happens that I have a taste for seafood: fish, shrimp, lobster -- things like that. I used to take my wife along now and then, back when I had a wife, before she died.

But now I suddenly thought of a little problem, a very little problem that most people would think hardly worth mentioning. Interestingly enough, the problem didn't arise when I had my wife with me, and wouldn't be arising now if she were still with me and going with me to Ellery's Restaurant. But she has died, so she does not live with me anymore. I am not sure where she has gone, whether up, down, or sidewise, but that's neither here nor there. Anyway she's not here. Let me explain:

I have always tried to follow socially and ethically correct behavior, being a properly brought-up young fellow. When I was young I was always taught that it is nice to leave a good tip for servants or waiters in a hotel or restaurant -- places like that -- but not if the service is rendered by the proprietor herself, or her husband. Now that is precisely the case that existed with Ellery's Restaurant.

You see, Ellery had sort of a quirk. He had all the prices on his menu ending in fifty cents. Thought it looked elegant. High class. And it always seemed that the total on my tab ended in fifty cents. Unusual, but nicer than the ubiquitous ninety-nine cents that is now so common. When my wife (RIP) was with me and each of our meals ended in fifty cents, the total would end in a round dollar and there would be no problem. "No problem," as young people all say today. The problem arose when it ended in fifty cents, because I don't like to carry change in my pocket. I would rather let it accumulate on the bedroom dresser. I wasn't able to round it off in a tip because I didn't tip Ellery because he was a friend and because he was the one who always served me. The result of all this is that sometimes I would leave Ellery's Restaurant still owing him fifty cents, and sometimes with his owing me fifty cents, which we would take into account the next time. I generally preferred to overpay him by the fifty cents, because I hate the feeling of owing people money. But fifty cents wasn't a whole lot, even back then, and my conscience was able to live with it, from one meal at Ellery's to the next.

I have a niece, a nice niece, who lives nearby and comes around from time to time to drink a can of Coca Cola or a glass of grapefruit juice from my refrigerator, check on me, and help a bit with some household chores that happened to have piled up -- that sort of thing. This morning when she came around, she stared at me and said I didn't look so good. Said I looked pale. Didn't say "deathly pale," but I could tell that's what she meant.

"What else is new," I replied rather smart-alecky. "I haven't looked good for twenty years, and have been pale for part of that time."

159

"I am serious," she said. "Let me take your pulse."

"All right, I said, take it, take all you want, but leave me some of it. I may need it."

"Ha ha, very funny. I told you I'm serious." So she took my pulse. Then she herself went pale, maybe almost as pale as I. "Your pulse is feeble," she said, trying to smile a friendly little smile. "I think you are going to die. It looks as though your time has come, Uncle Don. No one can live forever," she continued, offering a soothing philosophical insight into man's mortality that I was already aware of. "And you have already lived more than your allotted span." I knew all that -- she didn't have to tell me. But women like to talk, you know.

"That's all right," I said. "You know who to call when I go. First my lawyer and then the funeral home. I'm ready."

Then I thought of something.

"No!" I exclaimed, suddenly raising my head an inch or two off the pillow. "I can't go yet. You have to DO something!"

"Don't get so excited," she said. "It's bad for you. Now what is it? Is something bothering you?"

"Give me artistic restoration or a long-lasting aspirin repository or something! Quick! Don't let me die!"

"What on earth is the matter with you? Don't you feel well? I thought you said just a minute ago that you were ready to die. What's gotten into you all of a sudden?"

"It's Ellery," I explained.

"Ellery?"

"Yes, Ellery. I can't die now, dammit. I still owe Ellery fifty cents."

THE END

Gamecocks

I live in a small state in the South where funny things can happen.

A few years ago some enterprising students and fans from the University of South Carolina got together and designed and printed up some T-shirts that immediately achieved great popularity and considerable fame, even notoriety. Although the shirts subsequently have often been copied and imitated, the originals are heirlooms today, and now sell for $150 to $200 or more each, if they can be found at all.

The story begins, not at the University of South Carolina, but on the campus of their mortal rivals, the Clemson Tigers. As chance and unexpected opportunities would have it, an attractive young coed got into some trouble with the Clemson authorities.

According to the headlines of the school newspaper, "The Tiger," known for its open reporting policy and broad-minded views, the young girl was accosted, paneled, and suspended for "engaging in improper activities at an improper place and time." The body of the story went on to explain that a vigilant watchman assigned to the Athletic Department was checking the condition of the men's showers and locker rooms one evening after a Saturday football game and found, to his surprise, chagrin, and horror, the aforementioned young coed in one of the

163

changing rooms giving her adored hero, the starting defensive left tackle, what was euphemistically known around the campus as a "Bill-Monica" job. Very crude, yes. In more refined circles it would have been called... well... a fellatio job. Yes. Right there in the bowels of the school's pristine athletic facilities of which the entire University was so proud.

The alert watchman was suddenly faced with a difficult climacteric decision, namely whether it would be more lucrative to accept the generous monetary gratuity offered by the young football player in return for silence on the matter, or to righteously and indignantly refuse it in anticipation of the possibly greater kudos he might gain from the Administration by helping to bring these perpetrators of naughty behaviour to justice, thereby solidifying his own position as a permanent member of the University staff until time for his retirement.

Fortunately, or unfortunately, depending upon how you view the matter, he chose the path of upright honesty and, speaking out of the side of his mouth -- for he had understandably turned his head away in modesty -- he explained to the young couple that he was compelled "to do his duty" (as "The Tiger" later quoted him as saying). In short, he turned them IN, and it wasn't long before the lovely maiden was OUT. "We will have no more of THAT," asseverated the Dean of Students and the University Provost almost in unison. Clemson's starting defensive left tackle was chastised, criticized, castigated, and cautioned, but was too important to be kicked out or even impeached -- too big to fail, you might say -- as he was the best defensive left tackle the Clemson squad had.

Not surprisingly, news of these exciting untoward events spread rapidly to the campus of the University of South Carolina Gamecocks. The dismay which the story brought to the Clemson campus was equaled only by the glee which it brought to the campus of USC. Now if you were a student of zoology and animal behavior, you would think that Tigers would have no trouble gobbling up Gamecocks on a regular basis. But in this case you would be wrong. For some years now, the Tigers had a poor record on the gridiron against their rivals, having won only one of the last five games.

It was the phrase "No more of THAT" that gave the USC activists their idea. They promptly put their heads together and got busy, for the annual Clemson-USC football game was only four weeks away. They developed their plan, organized their supporters, and got to work. When game time came, they were ready.

As soon as the park opened, they unfolded several giant banners, which they paraded around the stadium entrances and parking lots. They set up a number of little stands to sell T-shirts with the new motto they had concocted. Altogether they had 12,000 T-shirts for sale at $25.00 each, $10.00 of which was to go to the benefit of the USC Athletic Department Scholarship Fund. The fans loved the little red and white shirts, and they were all sold out before the end of the half-time break and the beginning of the third quarter.

During the second half, the South Carolina fans began to chant, "We will lick your Tigers, we will lick your Tigers." Fortunately USC did win that game, but it was close.

Oh, by the way, the motto on the banners and T-shirts read:

YOU CAN'T LICK OUR COCKS

Some of the more extroverted USC students and fans had even underlined the word <u>our</u> on their T-shirts with a heavy black marking pen.

YOU CAN'T LICK <u>OUR</u> COCKS

THE ORIGINAL END

Epilogue

Now the authorities in South Carolina, including both the Governor of the State and the USC Dean of Students, promptly declared that sales of the popular T-shirts would be restricted because they were in bad taste (even though by then all of the shirts had been sold).

Whether or not influenced by the events of that memorable afternoon, some years later the South Carolina State legislature judiciously considered a bill proposing a change in the name of the USC mascot, in view of the fact that gamecock fighting was now illegal in South Carolina. I thereupon took it upon myself to write a letter to the editor of my local newspaper saying I believed that organized tiger fighting in South Carolina also was illegal, as well as fighting of cougars, lions, wildcats, panthers, and bearcats, not to mention bulldogs and riverdogs, all of which are South Carolina mascots. I don't know if the legislators ever read my letter, but fortunately the bill never

166

passed. Otherwise we would have no one left to do our fighting for us on the gridiron but Generals, Cavaliers, Patriots, Trojans, and of course Rebels. And who wants to go back to "Gone with the Wind" days anyway?

THE FINAL END

Remembering Guernica

"*Yo me acuerdo de Guernica*," he said, in clear Spanish, with a slight foreign accent. I remember Guernica.

"I thought you just told me you had never been to Spain."

"I remember it, as I said, although I never actually set foot in that country," he cryptically replied.

*   *   *   *   *

This strange exchange of words came up in a conversation during the luncheon break at a big meeting in Washington D.C. a number of years ago, back in the late sixties.

Maybe you have read about Franco's devastation of the Basque town of Guernica in the Spanish Civil War. I learned about it in school. The notoriety of Guernica was later spread worldwide with the gruesome picture of the horrors of war painted by Pablo Picasso. You can still see "Guernica" today in the Picasso Museum in Paris, on the rue Thorigny not far from the Place de la Bastille. With the help of Adolf Hitler's bombers, Francisco Franco leveled Guernica in April 1937, as an example, to show the Basques and other Loyalists still resisting him that he meant business.

*   *   *   *   *

169

Of course, there are a lot of meetings going on in Washington all the time, meetings between all sorts of people and organizations and government officials and big businessmen and lobbyists and I don't know what all. Sometimes you find unusual people at these meetings.

The occasion I have in mind was a meeting of the WMO -- the World Meteorological Organization. Meteorological means weather. I was a junior officer, a flunky really, working at the Department of State in its beautiful building on 23rd Street, just a couple of blocks up from the Lincoln Memorial. "New State" it was affectionately called. In many of the big international organizations the practice is for one or another of the member governments to serve as host for the periodic meetings. The honor of being host may rotate among the members. This time it was the turn of the United States to host the meeting of the WMO. It is the Department of State (which is what we call our Foreign Office) that handles such matters.

Not everybody knows what the Department of State is, or even that it exists. (Someone once asked me what I did for a living, and I simply replied that I worked for the Department of State. I thought that would answer the question, but apparently it did not. She thereupon asked, "Oh, that's interesting... which state?" I choked a little, and even thought of replying, "the state of confusion" or some such smarty answer, but managed to hold my tongue. However, all that is beside the point.)

My job at the time was to help make arrangements for this kind of international meetings. It involved schedules, agendas, interpreters, sound equipment, seating, security, participants, accreditations, food and refreshments, representatives, experts, press relations, and other administrative details. Of course I wasn't the only one handling all of this; there were a few other young officers assigned to the task, and some senior ones too. We were all quite serious.

The subjects discussed in these WMO meetings were generally very technical as well as numerous and varied: coordination with aviation needs and requirements, compatibility of sensors and weather recording devices, collaboration in the use of shared data, standardization of collection techniques around the world, improvement of forecasts through studies of correlation between predictions and outcomes, and connections with scientific companies producing atmospheric measurement and observation equipment, and many other matters of concern.

Being just a flunky, or gopher, as some of us proudly called ourselves, I was not involved in the substance of these meetings, which would have been way over my head. What was most interesting to me, however, was the variety of fascinating people that turned up at gatherings like this.

I guess it was during a coffee break that, because I speak Spanish, I struck up a conversation with one of the foreign representatives from South America. This one was from Venezuela, but he had a certain accent that I didn't recognize. My Spanish was pretty good, although not quite perfect, and this fellow was inquisitive enough to ask me where I had learned the language. I explained that I had studied Spanish in school before coming to work for the

Department of State, but that I had also spent some time working in Spain, which had given me the opportunity to practice and improve my command of the language.

Now it was my turn, and I asked him where *he* was from. He told me Caracas, adding, rather cryptically, that he "had never actually been in Spain." Now I had never been to Caracas; in fact, I had never been south of Mexico. But I know that there are dialects or regional accents in parts of various Spanish-speaking countries, just as there are various dialects in English and other languages all over the world.

However, something didn't seem quite right. Although his Spanish was excellent, his accent didn't sound as though it had come from some odd corner of South America; it somehow sounded more continental to me. So, curious but not wanting to embarrass him, I gently asked, "Have you always lived in Caracas?"

"No," he said, "I was born and grew up in Germany." Ah, that explains it, I thought. "But," he continued, "I have lived in Venezuela for over twenty years now." He then told me that his career in meteorology grew out of his interest in airplanes and love of flying. He had flown planes in Germany in his younger days, but the conditions and opportunities in Venezuela after World War II looked more inviting and propitious, so he emigrated and had been living in Caracas virtually ever since. He was now working for the government as an official of the Venezuelan Weather Service, competent in his work and happy in his life. He was an intelligent and pleasant fellow, interesting to talk to. His Spanish was a bit scholarly, but easy to understand,

172

easier than the speech of some natives who can be almost incomprehensible when they get going fast with each other.

"Well," I said, "you certainly speak beautiful Spanish now; I almost thought you were born in Venezuela."

"Thank you," he said. "You speak Spanish very well too. What part of Spain did you live in?"

I told him I had lived for a couple of years in Bilbao, in the Basque Country. Some people have heard of the Basque Country who have never heard of Bilbao, even though Bilbao is, or was, the fifth or sixth largest city in Spain. He seemed genuinely interested, as I spoke about other towns and places near Bilbao that I knew or had visited. For instance, I used to swim on the beaches at Neguri and Algorta; I had crossed the hanging bridge to Portugalete; I had visited the war memorial in Guernica. I loved the quaint fishing port of Munguía, and I used to see *jai alai* games in nearby Durango, which I explained was only 40 kilometers east of Bilbao. I was astonished when he said, "No, it's more like 60 kilometers from Bilbao."

"How can you know that?" I asked in surprise. I thought you said you had never been to Spain."

"Durango is 25 kilometers south southwest of Guernica," he replied.

"Do you know about Guernica?" I asked in wonder. "Guernica was destroyed during the Spanish Civil War."

"I know it only from the aerial charts: Durango and Guernica and those other places were points on the map to me. Or simply coordinates, actually. Guernica is the one I remember best."

I was beginning to get the picture. "Then you have seen Guernica and those other towns from the air? Is that it? Were you making aerial photographs or something?"

"Not exactly. I was a pilot in the Luftwaffe," he replied. "It's where we tried out the new Stuka dive-bombers."

And he was such a nice chap.

THE END

Conversion

"Is anything wrong with you?"

"No, there's nothing wrong with me," he said. But her question started him thinking.

* * * * *

Abner lived in an ordinary little town; he came from an ordinary family; he lived in an ordinary neighborhood; and he went to an ordinary school. He had grown up with a younger brother and sister, and with two loving parents. Nothing surprising there.

All of this was in south central Tennessee, in the middle of what was affectionately known as "The Bible Belt." Abner's family and all the people is his neighborhood, and most of the rest of the town as well, attended church religiously. Around town there were a considerable number of various denominations to choose from, as one might surmise, although to an outsider there seemed little difference among most of them in their beliefs, practices, organizations, and functions. Church activities there were a big part of people's lives and, for many, were their principal interest outside of their jobs and their children's schooling.

As a young lad, Abner dutifully went along to church with his family, although it wasn't long before he began to have doubts and to realize he didn't believe all that stuff.

He had read somewhere that a person who "didn't believe all that stuff" was called an Atheist, and thereupon decided that an Atheist was what he wanted to be. He was pleased to learn that, in spite of its sound, "Atheist" really didn't have anything to do with "anarchist" or "terrorist."

The other outstanding thing about Abner was his keen interest in the opposite sex, especially girls. Abner's developing passion for the idea of romance started when he was very young, indeed in knee pants, and grew rapidly during his high school years, along with the realization that he was an Atheist at heart. Abner had quit going to church, to his parents' chagrin, although they were broad minded enough to feel no one should be required to attend church against his will.

The girls liked Abner too. He was an attractive young man. By the time he got out of high school he was, to all outward appearances, what the girls would call "a good catch." He had gotten a job soon after graduation, and was working for the local newspaper, running the presses and helping with general maintenance work. Girls married young in Tennessee in those days, and Abner was very eligible.

Abner didn't go around talking about his religious beliefs, or his lack of religious beliefs. He didn't think that was necessary. Although he was no genius, he was wise enough to realize -- all this being in the Bible Belt -- wise enough to realize that it might scare some of his female prospects away if he were to get on the subject of all the impossible stuff that is packed into the Bible and into religion. He would discretely try to keep it to himself. But he couldn't. He couldn't hide it. It didn't take more than two or three dates for a prospective lady-friend to find out that Abner was an Atheist. An Atheist indeed. A Non-Believer.

But after two or three dates Abner also thought he should start getting some reward for the money he had been putting into dating this girl or that girl, money for movies, money for popcorn, money for coca-cola and sometimes even a beer, money for gas to drive to the beach, and money to buy a sandwich on the way back.

These two circumstances always seemed to come at the same time: just as Abner began to feel the moment was right to move on to some serious physical intimacy, the girl would learn of his negative religious views and call it off before it ever got started. Abner was getting nowhere. You see, all the girls in his town were well brought up, and were brought up to love our Lord Jesus Christ and follow His teaching, and to shun atheists and naughty boys who only wanted one thing, especially if the naughty boys were atheists as well.

They called Abner an infidel and told him to get his hands off them and take them home.

One of the girls he liked told him blatantly that she could never let an Atheist make love to her. "What if we had a baby? He might turn out to be a little Devil," she said, with a note of serious concern in her voice, "even if we were married," she added, to drive the point home.

177

That went on for a couple of years. Abner was now in his mid-twenties and his romantic urges were bursting to find a satisfying outlet. "This can't go on," he declared to himself one frustrating Saturday night. Then one day he happened to be reading a book of famous quotations. One of them, attributed to old Senator Watson from Indiana, was "If you can't beat 'em, join 'em." That started him thinking, and gave him ideas.

So he decided to take another look at church. That seemed to be where both the problem and the rewards lay. Maybe the church could be the pathway both to eternal happiness with Christ our Savior, up in Heaven, and to infernal happiness with women and their favors down here on Earth. Maybe there is something to be said for our Lord Jesus Christ after all. People wouldn't have to know I still don't believe He walked on water and made wine out of a rock and all that stuff. Maybe I can just pretend, or maybe I could even keep my mouth shut if I tried hard enough.

So Abner kept his mouth shut and started going to church again, something he had not done since he was ten or twelve years old. The recrudescence was not difficult for him; it was easy to slip back into the swing of things, the routine of the old rituals, the repetition of the prayers, and the familiarity of the traditional hymns. He liked the hymns the best, for with the hymns you could think of the music part, the notes and the melodies and the harmonies, and not have to think too much about the words that went along with them. And he began to feel or realize that his new attendance at church gave him a fresh attractiveness in the eyes of the young ladies at coffee hour after the Sunday services and at the Wednesday-night suppers.

178

At first, Abner only went through the motions of belief and prayer and repentance and the other outward and visible signs of being a Christian, just following the same things that other people around him seemed to be doing. He stood up when they stood up, and he sat down when they sat down. (In the Episcopal Church there is a lot of standing up and sitting down.) And he said "and with thy spirit" and "Amen" when they did. Some of the people around him crossed themselves from time to time, and some of them didn't. So Abner crossed himself half the time; that seemed about right.

This went on for quite a while. It is amazing what practice and repetition can do. Although it seems like a miracle, gradually the exposure to the teachings of Christ and proximity to the fellowship of His followers in this warm little family church began to make their mark on Abner. The Church life and routine that he had factitiously forced himself into was having an effect. Hard as it is to believe, Abner was becoming a Believer, even if he had not quite yet achieved the unquestioning apodictic faith of the holiest among them. Nevertheless, he did actually begin to believe some of the things he had just been mouthing with lip service and doing by rote. And while this was happening he had been getting very friendly with some of the girls he found in the congregation. Then once again, two developments occurred at approximately the same time.

Abner started dating one or two of the prettiest and sexiest girls he had met there. When he took them out for supper or a drive occasionally, they decided they really liked this good-looking ephebus. Indeed, several of the young ladies found that he had stirred up their romantic inclinations and juices to the point that they were ready to try him out. Girls have hormones and urges too, you know -- it's not just boys. They started making suggestions and even advances toward this attractive young man who had begun to captivate their hearts. It was just the situation that Abner had been hoping for and longing for all these many months and years.

There was one girl he especially liked -- her name was Pearle. Pearle enjoyed playing an old card game called cribbage, and taught Abner to play too. It was a card game for two -- perhaps that is why she chose it. Abner caught on quickly, for it helped to bring him closer to this sweet maiden. Pearle could see that Abner could see that there were other things to see in her besides what you could actually see. She knew that he could see her looking at him watching her when she wiggled a bit. So she liked playing cribbage, this game for two, in order to be alone with him. Then one evening at her place she gave him a kiss and said she wanted to play another game.

"One more game of cribbage?" said Abner, logically but naïvely. "Sure, why not?"

"Well, no... another game... maybe something else," said the damsel with a smile, caressing the back of Abner's neck with her left hand while keeping her right hand in ready reserve. She stood up from the card table, smoothed down her skirt, and slowly started drifting toward the bedroom, diaphanous as Lucia di Lammermoor.

Now Abner was a bright boy for his size, so immediately, or almost immediately, he began to suspect what she was driving at. "Do you mean...?" said Abner, his voice trailing off in a mixture of surprise and shock.

"Well, we are both adults, practically, aren't we? And we are both capable of consenting, aren't we?" she said, turning and smiling gently into his eyes while holding out her hand to him -- both hands actually.

"No no," cried Abner, as his image of the horror she was suggesting struck with a flash upon his inward eye. "We can't do anything like that."

"Why not?" said Pearle, moving ever closer. "Is anything wrong with you?"

"No, nothing is wrong with me."

"Well then?"

"What would Jesus say? Jesus wouldn't like it at all."

"He wouldn't have to know."

"But He *would* know. Jesus knows everything. We... duh... We just can't. It would be adultery. You know, the Seventh Commandment and all that... from the Sermon on the Mount... Sorry."

THE ORIGINAL END

Epilogue

The next day, after doing some research, Pearle called Abner on her cell phone and straightaway said, "No, it wouldn't be... Neither of us is married."

Abner was silent for half a minute, possibly thinking.

"Oh...?" he finally said, perking up, although his voice still sounded somewhat confused.

THE FINAL END

Good Luck

Billy O'Dell and Darrell Phillips were the best of friends. They grew up in the same neighborhood, went to the same Sunday School when they were little, and played games with the same group of neighborhood kids. Billy, an only child, was three months older than Darrell, and thought of him almost as his little brother. Darrell had two older sisters who liked to push him around and tell him what to do, so he valued Billy's companionship from a very early age.

Billy and Darrell were in fact related -- distant cousins -- although neither knew that for many years. They had the same great-great... (five times great) grandfather, Hugh Drayton, and each had descended from one of Hugh's two sons, Thomas and Percival. Thomas and Percival Drayton achieved a certain degree of notoriety as senior officers fighting on opposite sides in the Civil War in the 1860's. /1

Maybe the common ancestry showed through, for the boys were like enough to be brothers, even twins. Their first disappointment was their separation into different classes in elementary school. Although they were close in age, Darrell's birthday was in October, missing the September cut-off date for six-year-olds entering first grade. So he was always a year behind Billy, all the way

/1 See "Pairing the Vote" in SHORT STORIES FOREVER, p 234.

through school, but he made up for it by studying hard and gaining the reputation of being the smartest boy in his class. But Billy was smart too, and they often talked with each other about their lessons. Both also liked the same sports, especially baseball and soccer, dated the same girls, and went to the same church, where they prayed to the same God and confessed their sins to the same priest.

As most people tended to do in those days, in due course they both married spouses of the opposite gender and even had some children. Their jobs took them to different states for a few years at a time, but nevertheless they kept in touch. Later on in life they returned to their birthplace and renewed their acquaintance and friendship in their final years.

Neither of the two men was immortal. The aches and pains of normal old age encroached upon them as upon all old people. In their late seventies, however, they found themselves with further afflictions, namely, cancer. Pancreatic cancer. Billy was the first to contract the malady. He had been suffering uncomfortable abdominal pains for three or four weeks when he decided to see his doctor. The prognosis was not good. He was told he had a life expectancy of nine months, which would probably mean three months in discomfort, three months in pain, and three months in agony, prior to blessed relief brought on by sweet death.

Darrell was concerned for the condition of his friend Billy, and even discussed with him the possibility of considering some means of bringing a final sweet end to the increasing pain and agony. They also discussed their

184

thoughts on these possibilities with their parish priest, who in no uncertain terms insisted that any such ideas were contrary to the will of God and the teachings of the Church. Besides, suicide was against the law; in some states it was a capital offense. Anyone who took his own life for whatever reason would never be accepted into Heaven, but must expect to go to Hell, or at least to Purgatory, for an indefinite period of time, maybe for eternity. "That's a tough decision," thought Billy, as his pain and agony were increasing daily. After seven months, when he had entered the third phase described by his doctor, he decided he could stand the pain and the agony no longer, although he still had an estimated two more months to go. He went back to his priest to ask him to try and find some means of acquiring a special dispensation, or of buying some "indulgences" that would allow him to end all his pain and suffering, but still be a Christian and still have a chance of getting into Heaven.

"There is really no way you can do *that*," the priest insisted. "Are you getting all the pain pills you need?" he suggested.

"Well, no," replied Billy. "I really want more. I would like to take a couple of dozen more, all at once, like my supply for the next two weeks, but they will only give me one at a time and won't let me save them up."

"And rightly so, my son. For you to take your life by swallowing too many pills would be almost as bad, in the eyes of God, as shooting yourself in the head with that WWII Luger pistol your father stole from the dead German during the Battle of the Bulge. Maybe even worse, for with the gun you might make it look like an accident."

"But Father, I am in pain. I mean agony. Actually both pain and agony mixed together, but I think it's mostly agony," said poor Billy.

"You have to grin and bear it, my son. God has his purpose in all things. It may be that His purpose is to make you a stronger person by placing a few obstacles and adversities in your path through life," said the kindly priest.

"I'm not talking about my path through life," said Billy. "I'm talking about the end of the road."

"Let me say a little prayer for you, my son."

"All right, go ahead. And I'll pray that your prayers will do some good."

So that's what they did. They prayed. But the pain didn't go away. It continued. Actually both the pain and the agony continued. But the good news is that Billy died one week before his date to go, one whole week without the pain and agony that he had expected and was his due. An extra week of Heavenly bliss, free of pain.

Now about a month before Billy died, something else happened. Darrell began to experience the same discomfort of incipient pancreatic cancer that Billy was already suffering from. Darrell's doctor gave him the same baleful prediction that he had so accurately given Billy. For the next few weeks Darrell suffered the double affliction of his own enervating pain and the distress of seeing his life-long friend suffer increasing agony as *his* life approached its end, however blessed as it was in the eyes of God, unsullied by further thoughts of suicide.

"I don't know how you can stand it," Darrell said as he tried to bring comfort to Billy's bedside. "If my own pain gets any worse I am going to go to Oregon to do something about it."

"To Oregon? Why Oregon?"

"Doctor Kevorkian. It's where Dr. Kevorkian has his clinic."

"Dr. Kevorkian?"

"Yes, Dr. Kevorkian. In Oregon compassionate assisted suicide is legal, and Dr. Kevorkian is the one who led the way. He is the one who can bring relief from pain and suffering. Lasting and permanent relief from the excruciating pain of pancreatic cancer that I know you must be suffering."

"Yes, I can understand your wanting to do that," said Billy from his bed of pain. "But, you know... God and the Church... "

"Yes, I know. But I am a coward. I would rather go to Hell and face the Fires of Gehenna than suffer any more of this hell on earth that I am beginning to feel, and that I know you are enduring so bravely. I have made a reservation to fly out to Portland next week."

But before next week arrived, his friend Billy was dead. I would like to say that he had a beatific smile on his face as he passed away.   Actually it was more of a ghastly grimace. His fists were clenched. His cheeks were sunken, and his front teeth had bitten halfway through his lower lip. However, these were all nugatory things that a good undertaker could easily fix right here on earth, fortunately. The important thing is that Billy went straight to Heaven. God, in His mercy and loving forbearance, did not even make Billy go through Purgatory. He had already been through enough right here on Earth.

Five days later Darrell boarded the plane for Portland, Oregon, as planned. He knew he would go to Hell for violating the will of God and the doctrines of the Church against suicide, but he was determined. Adamant. He had even sometimes wondered whether Hell actually existed. Now he would find out. Nowadays not many people who went to Hell ever came back to describe the experience. Virgil and Dante, perhaps, but they were the exceptions; I don't think Eurydice ever made it back quite all the way.

So he took off from the airport that Sunday after early mass, his last and final mass -- his last supper, so to speak, although for him it was breakfast. The three-hour time difference was to his advantage: he was scheduled into the Portland airport in mid-afternoon and was to present himself at Dr. Kevorkian's clinic at 10:00 am the next morning.

* * * * *

Now, already up in Heaven, Billy was meeting some of his old friends, the few who had led the purest and holiest lives, and even some of his ancestors who had fought in the Civil War. Paradoxical as it seems, whether they had been with the North or with the South, all the old soldiers were confident that God was on their side. Perhaps God, like so many other people in America at the time, did not know which side he really should support, so He remained neutral, or supported both sides, a difficult position to hold, but a relief from the burden of having to make a decision.

Then a surprising thing happened.

Billy had not been in Heaven very long when he met a group of new arrivals, and much to his astonishment there was his dear friend Darrell Phillips right in the middle of them. "Darrell," cried Billy, overcome with delight and surprise, "is that really you?"

"Well, here I am," said Darrell, "in the flesh... Well, maybe not in the flesh... I shouldn't have said that... but at least I am here in spirit."

"Yes, I can see that. You do look in good spirits, a little pale perhaps. But tell me... how in Hell... I mean, how on Earth... did you make it? I wouldn't have thought you had the ghost of a chance after taking your own life. That's not supposed to be allowed here. Did you buy some special indulgences I didn't know about? Or didn't you go see Dr. Kevorkian in Oregon?"

"I was going, but then I had a stroke of luck."

"A stroke of luck? What kind of luck?"

"I got on the airplane as planned, a Boeing 717, one of the smaller jets with only 127 total, passengers and crew."

"All right. Then what?"

"We ran into a violent thunderstorm over southern Montana, right near the Big Sky ski resort that your friend Chet Huntley used to run."

"I only knew Chet a little; I dated Tippy a few times before he married her. What did you do, jump out and go skiing? They used to describe that place as heavenly."

"Very good. Ha ha. Actually you may be thinking of a place in California, on Lake Tahoe, called Heavenly Valley. Anyway, I didn't have to jump out. The plane lost control in a downdraft and ran right into a mountainside, where I lost my life -- what I still had of it -- along with 126 other people. All 127 killed instantly."

"That doesn't sound very lucky."

"It wasn't, for the other 126, but for me it was a God-send, so to speak. It let me get to Heaven, still in the state of grace, without having to violate anybody's laws against suicide. Apparently merely lusting in one's heart for suicide is not a punishable offense," said Darrell in his philosophical tone of voice. "And it's certainly rather nice here," he added, looking around. "Have you seen anybody else you know?"

THE END

Consummation

The Peabody Institute and the Julliard School are two of the best -- and certainly the best known -- music schools in the United States, although there are also other fine music schools such as Eastman and Curtis that are right up there with the top ones.

Rachael Portmann had always wanted to go to Julliard, but couldn't get in because of a technicality. It seems there were too many aspiring pianists knocking on the door at that time, and Julliard likes to keep a balanced, broad spectrum among its student body. Any one class from Julliard could have practically constituted a whole orchestra. So she went to Peabody to develop her musical talents, "majoring" in Piano.

Ruby Dubois liked to sing, and had shown considerable talent as a young child. At first she was not particularly interested in serious musical studies, but her father was a cellist and was on the faculty at Peabody. He had certain aspirations for his daughter, and his position offered a virtually tuition-free scholarship for faculty children. So Ruby went along with Peabody -- if not Peabody she would have had to go to the University of Maryland.

In due course Rachael and Ruby met as students at Peabody and found they had interests and talents that dovetailed nicely.

191

Actually it was not at Peabody that the two first met. A few years earlier, when Rachael was only fifteen and a half and Ruby was fourteen, they met at Mrs. Shippen's Dancing School in the suburbs of Washington, D.C. The parents of the girls did not know each other, but had similar ideas about the proper upbringing of their daughters as young ladies. These ideas included ballroom dancing lessons, which, while somewhat archaic, were believed to instill confidence and social grace into the deportment and bearing of young ladies, as well as physical grace and dexterity in learning how to put their best foot forward, so to speak.

The first thing the two young ladies realized that they had in common was their height. Rachael was almost five feet ten and Ruby was already five feet eight and a half, which made each of them half a head taller than most of the boys, who at that age had not yet begun to sprout. Usually Rachael did not mind looking down on boys, as it were, but when it came to dancing it was a different matter. She did not always like the feeling that, when she was dancing with a boy and looking over his head, he didn't often look into her eyes, or even at her chin, but seemed to look spontaneously straight ahead into the top of her ball gown, her dancing dress, with its properly fitted, slightly décolleté, stylish, neckline. "What do you think you are looking at?" Rachael once blurted out, upsetting decorum in one corner of the hall, to the embarrassment of the boy and the chagrin of the dancing teacher, not to mention the great amusement of all the other young people within earshot, especially the young gentlemen.

Being two of the tallest in the dancing class, Rachael and Ruby also found themselves paired off together on more than one occasion. In spite of the efforts of the school's administrators to keep the ratio of boys to girls fifty-fifty, there were usually a few more girls than boys. Sometimes a couple of naughty boys would skip class and slip off to catch a movie down the street during the two-hour dancing session, skewing the gender ratio even further. As a result, the two girls were singled out because of their height and told to dance together, periodically alternating the rôle of boy and girl, or leader and follower. They didn't seem to mind; they took it all in good stride, so to speak. They even found something to giggle about, especially on the slow dances. They were amused when they realized that the fronts of their dresses, where their budding breasts were beginning to stick out a little, naturally bumped together. Although Rachael was somewhat taller than Ruby, her shoulder straps were longer, just enough to put their points of contact at the same level. Very interesting. As Rachael was leading, her right point of contact brushed perfectly against Ruby's left one. To add to the interest of the contact, Ruby would wiggle her shoulders slightly from right to left, and was delighted to see Rachael pick up on the idea and return the wiggle and the friction. The girls thought this little game of theirs was hilarious, and they giggled as they wiggled, almost laughing out loud, confusing and disturbing the dancing mistress who didn't understand and was mystified by this minor disruption of proper decorum.

After dancing school, several years went by before the girls saw each other again.

Rachael had a younger brother, Harry. When they were very young, Rachael, like most elder sisters, enjoyed bossing little Harry around and telling him what do to. As Harry got older he began to resist being pushed around by his sister. When she realized she could no longer beat him, Rachael joined him and his friends, that is to say in games and sports. She could run and jump with the best of them, especially with her eighteen-month age advantage. She thereupon became something of a tomboy, as they were called in those days. In spite of her love of the out-of-doors, her father, a bit of a pianist himself, insisted upon her having piano lessons from the time she was six years old. She found it boring at first, but in the third grade she had an opportunity to perform in a school show. She liked it and liked showing off so much that she thereafter pursued her music studies as assiduously as possible.

Ruby, meanwhile, grew up as an only child, beloved and spoiled by doting parents and a number of female cousins who lived nearby and let her play house and dolls and dress-up with them. The girls also used to sing children's songs together, but it soon became evident that the most talented of the bunch was young Ruby. Ruby always loved to sing, and it was because of the opportunities for singing that she became a faithful member of the Baptist Church, where everybody loves music and loves to sing whether they know how to or not. She joined the choir and attended service more regularly than her parents ever had done.

Otherwise the early lives of these two young women were relatively uneventful and not too different from each other, until they got to Peabody and met again. At Peabody they renewed their old acquaintance, and more. They were delighted to learn how their musical interests and prospective careers complemented each other. They began performing together at school, and in their senior year accepted some engagements to perform off campus for the New Metropolitan Baptist Church, the Baltimore Music Guild, and other organizations of local music lovers, splitting the modest fees they earned. They even opened a joint bank account as they excitedly planned a musical career together.

After graduation and receipt of their music degrees, they continued their partnership, got an agent, further developed their routine, and went around the country on a concert tour. Their favorite venue was San Francisco, where they first performed at the Presidio Officers' Club, and some months later at the Performing Arts Center, and ultimately at the grand Davies Symphony Hall downtown. They loved California and its friendly atmosphere, and decided to make it their home. They bought a modest apartment on Donahue Street in Sausalito. They would expand their horizons and tour the world, but now had their home and San Francisco to come back to.

They both loved the classical *lieder*, or love songs, of Schumann and Schubert, and later those of Richard Strauss and Hugo Wolf as well. In due course they added songs of Liszt and Mendelssohn because the accompanying piano parts were more challenging for Rachael. They felt like "stout Cortez" discovering the Pacific Ocean when they came upon some of the love songs of Benjamin Britten. Two of their special favorites were Britten's "Winter Words" and "My Beloved Is Mine." They pictured themselves as female images of the famous musical duo, pianist Benjamin Britten and his beloved companion, tenor Peter Pears. They were not only amused but quite pleased when the musical reviews noticed the parallel and began to refer to them as a couple in the same image as Britten and Pears. The parallel was evident, and apt, and did not bother the young women at all. In fact, they rather liked it. Furthermore, times had changed in the last fifty years, and there were now opportunities open to them that their heroes, Britten and Pears, could only have dreamed of. There was something now available that was never an option for Britten and Pears, namely, same-sex marriage. After all, the two young women had for several months been sharing facilities, bank accounts, earrings, hats, lipstick, deodorant, bedrooms and, if necessary, even beds, especially when they were on tour, and sometimes even when they were not.

The next time their concert tour schedule brought them back to California, they did it. It was September, 2008. They got married, along with 4,000 other California same-gender couples bursting through the glass doors that year, when such unions had just become legal. As an outward and visible sign of their inward and spiritual love and devotion, they both modified their names slightly. Each took a piece of the other's name and added it to her own. Rachael became Rachael Ruby Portmann, and Ruby became Ruby Rachael Dubois. However, they did not have their agent make these changes on their public notices and program announcements -- that might be too confusing.

Their agent was able to arrange several concert tours in Europe, where, interestingly enough, it was easier to get good bookings in fine concert halls than in the United States. The governments of most European countries are far more generous in their support of the arts than is the case in the USA. The duo performed in Germany in places like the gorgeous Bamberg Concert Hall, the *Badisches Staatstheater* in Karlsruhe, and even the famous Victoria Hall in Geneva, where Peter Pears had so often sung accompanied by Benjamin Britten. Europeans especially loved Ruby -- her light lyric soprano voice and her lovely, demure, personality. She was an agreeable person and soon a favorite of the media, who were inclined to give her prominence over her companion in their reviews. Sometimes Rachael's name did not even appear in the local newspaper reports, and she was understandably annoyed to see herself occasionally referred to merely as "Ruby Dubois's accomplished accompanist." But she would pretend that her joy was to see and encourage Ruby's growing success and increasing popularity. Pretend.

Ruby, more than Rachael, also attracted male admirers who wanted to take her out to dinner, or buy her drinks, or engage her for private musical seances or interludes. Although the press did not mind reporting that Ruby and Rachael were a couple, and even enjoyed doing so, some men were reluctant to accept it, and Ruby regularly got propositions, often from older men, even married men. One man propositioned her insisting he was divorced. Our Ruby did not believe in divorce, and told him so. Now, to show you how far some men will go, this fellow, so taken by Ruby, offered to remarry his ex-wife if Ruby would go out with him, for then he would no longer be divorced. Although many Germans are quite intelligent, or are supposed to be, he was slow catching on to the fact that she was not interested in dating men. She was happy with her Rachael and in any case was too busy with her career for such nonsense. Maybe if things were different -- she politely said -- things would be different. But they weren't. Things weren't different.

At first Rachael was happy to see Ruby's popularity and fame grow and spread, proud of her own rôle in helping Ruby to develop her talents and public relations. However, after a while Rachael began to resent being eased out of the spotlight herself. She started pushing Ruby to accept musical pieces in which the piano played a more dominant rôle. In Schumann's gentle and affectionate *lieder* that the two of them had so loved in their early days together, she began to interpret her part as accompanist differently, bursting forth with unwritten *bravado* at unexpected moments, demonstrating her power and mastery of her instrument to the detriment of the lyrical voice she was supposed to be gently following and supporting.

Ruby, tolerant and loving person that she was, at first ignored these musical *ad liberatum* outbursts of her dear Rachael. She loved Rachael -- she really did -- and she could not bring herself to criticize her loved one's playing. Not for quite a while. Then one week when they were performing an engagement at the *Teatro Goldoni* in Florence, Rachael fell ill. She had caught a bug, had a mild fever and an intestinal upset. She proposed canceling the remaining four days of their engagement, but the Promoter was not so lightly inclined to lose the audience he foresaw coming to hear "*La Gioiella*" sing -- as the Italians had nicknamed Ruby -- "the Little Jewel." He arranged for another accompanist as a replacement, a pianist by the name of Hans Richter, who was a music teacher in a one-year residence at the *Istituto Europeo* right there in Florence, and, being German, was already familiar with about three quarters of the pieces on the program. Ruby was agreeable, although Rachael, even in her sickbed back at the hotel, didn't like the idea very much. She would be further than ever from the limelight. Out of it. Ruby dutifully arranged with the hotel concierge to bring in a doctor, who gave Rachael a mild antibiotic and some aspirin, and furthermore engaged a nurse to sit with her in her absence. But Ruby felt obligated to their contract -- the show must go on.

So that's what happened. Richter played gently and sensitively, as though he had been playing with Ruby for months -- like Rachael had played in their early days together. Ruby was amazed, and of course delighted. She had not dreamed that she could ever be comfortable with anyone but Rachael accompanying her, so close had they become in recent years. For the first time in her life, she realized that Rachael was not indispensable; not essential to her career. There were other pianists out there, and maybe some of them, like Mr. Richter, were not so pushy and domineering. In short, Ruby began to think of splitting from Rachael.

There was only one problem: Ruby did not believe in divorce. Her Church opposed it. Her Bible opposed it. Her religious upbringing opposed it. And her respect for marriage vows and sense of commitment opposed it. She would have to think of something else. Perhaps a legal separation would do, at least for a while. She couldn't remember whether the Bible said anything about legal separation. Perhaps no news is good news.

When they next got back to California, Ruby decided to go ahead and face the music -- so to speak. She went to a marriage counselor who was also a divorce attorney and a notary public and a few other things. They worked out a scenario that seemed best to satisfy Ruby's quandary and resolve her conflicted situation.

Ruby declared that they were going to court, much to Rachael's disgruntlement and dismay. Although Rachael did not like playing second fiddle -- so to speak -- to Ruby's sparkling singing career, she was perspicacious enough to realize that it had been a good thing for her too, and that she had gone further, and had become better known and even richer, by being Ruby's accompanist than she ever would have been by trying to strike out on her own as a concert pianist. She had talked this over with their agent, and that was her view too.

So they went to court. Rachael planned to contend that there were no grounds for divorce. No one had been "unfaithful," and they were certainly compatible. Ruby could not claim physical or mental abuse. Rachael felt sure that any reasonable judge would see it her way and reject any grounds for divorce that her dear Ruby might trump up.

Rachael confronted Ruby with all these points in an unsuccessful attempt to dissuade her from her plans to pursue the separation. Ruby was slipping out from under her control. Nothing like this had ever happened before, and Rachael couldn't understand it. Ruby had everything;

it was she, Rachael, who had every right to be the aggrieved one, what with Ruby racing ahead and stealing the limelight whenever possible when they performed together. Rachael had put time and energy into choosing program pieces for them to perform, into details of their concert schedules and arrangements, and even the plans for their food and lodging when they were on tour or in their little Sausalito apartment. She loved her dear Ruby and their arrangement, and used to say that she even would have loved her by any other name as well.

Ruby retorted that they could still see each other as often as they liked even after they were separated, if they wanted to, but that for the first time in her life she needed some independence. Rachael was dismayed, but saw nothing more that she could do beyond telling the judge that there were no grounds for divorce.

So they went to court.

* * * * *

THE JUDGE State your name, please.

RUBY Ruby, your Honor.

JUDGE Your whole name, please.

RUBY Ruby Rachael Dubois. But I don't...

JUDGE And who is this young lady with you?

RUBY She is my husband, your Honor.

JUDGE Your *husband*?

RUBY Yes, your Honor. Her Name is Rachael Ruby Portmann.

JUDGE She can tell me what her name is, thank you. What is your name?

RACHAEL It's just what she said, your Honor. Rachael Ruby Portmann.

JUDGE Your names are similar.

RACHAEL Yes, your Honor. We took each other's name as a middle name when we were married two years ago. Right here in California.

JUDGE How sweet.

RUBY Yes, we thought so too. That was the idea.

RACHAEL Then she put a frog in my bed.

RUBY Actually it was *our* bed.

RACHAEL But my side.

JUDGE Why would you do a thing like that?

RUBY I wanted to wake her up.

JUDGE Wake her up?

RUBY I was lonely.

REBECCA But she doesn't have any grounds for divorce, your Honor. We have always been compatible, no neglect or abuse, and we love each other.

RUBY Who said anything about divorce?

JUDGE This is a divorce court. You're not filing for divorce?

RUBY No, your Honor.

JUDGE Then what are you doing here today, taking up my time?

RUBY I am filing for an annulment, your Honor.

JUDGE Annulment?

RUBY Yes, your Honor.

JUDGE On what grounds?

RUBY Our marriage was never consummated, your Honor.

At that point the judge dropped his glasses. He managed to bend over and pick them up and put them back on his nose.

JUDGE I see.

THE END

Justifiable

It was all over the newspapers -- front-page news in the *Madison Capital Times* and even the *Milwaukee Journal Sentinel*.

CROSS PLAINS WOMAN ALLEGEDLY STRANGLED IN HER HOME

FOUL PLAY SUSPECTED

MOTIVE AND M.O. UNKNOWN

Well, maybe those reporters and editors didn't know what the motive and the M.O. were, but I did. You see, I was the alleged killer. I was also the real killer, although I am not an habitual criminal. I am not a criminal by birth or by genes, or by any sub-standard ghetto upbringing, or by political or religious persuasion. I am a killer by normal human behavior and by normal human instincts and emotions. I only did what any red-blooded man -- any white man that is -- would do under the circumstances. You see, I am the husband of the deceased. No, that's not quite right -- you can't be the husband of a dead person. I am the widower, the surviving spouse. I *had* been her husband. Let me tell you how it came to pass.

I supposed it all started when I got married. If I hadn't gotten married to Virginia it never would have happened. Virginia Eisennagel was my second wife, and my best one,

-- I'll say that for her -- although we didn't have any children. At least I don't think we did. I do have a son, Robert, by my first wife, though. Robert is now out of high school and running his own auto repair shop. He has always loved cars and loves his independence, although I still help him a bit financially from time to time. I also have a younger brother, Eric, living in Chicago, happily married, model husband and father.

Virginia was younger than I was. She was in a hurry to get married as soon as she could, after she got out of school, and I was available. She wanted to change her name as soon as possible, and I guess that's understandable. My name is Grunewald -- Lars Grunewald -- which may be a little better than Eisennagel, even if not much.

Virginia and I always wanted children too, but we were married for eight years before she finally got pregnant. It must have happened last July or August, just after I got back from a month-long business trip to Denmark. I am vice president of a company that makes cheese, and I am responsible for Development of Foreign Sales. We live in Cross Plains, a small town of half farmers and half commuters twenty miles west of Madison, where the company offices are.

My wife, Virginia, was born in West Point, Virginia, which is interesting because that is not far from Stratford, where ancestors of mine, the Lees, also held forth. She had Lees in her family too. We were not descended from Robert E. Lee, but were related to him. It was just after the Civil War, with its utter chaos and devastation, that "my" Lees came to Wisconsin -- not long after Wisconsin was admitted to the Union -- to start a new life in a new land, after their old way of life had been uprooted, burned out, and destroyed. Some of our Lee relatives also went to Brazil, where, deep in the hinterland a hundred miles north of Sao Paolo, they started a new community called Americana, now a bustling city of 200,000. But neither Virginia nor I liked the Lees very much. Abraham Lincoln was the one we loved, our greatest president. If Robert E. Lee had accepted Lincoln's offer to take command of the Union Army in May 1861, the War would have been over in four months instead of four years. Likewise, neither Virginia nor I liked Lee's attitude toward slavery very much. Lee thought slavery was all right if you treated your slaves kindly and as long as you gave some of them their freedom -- before they died -- and didn't make their iron shackles too tight. Although it seems rather macabre and scuzzy, and I don't know how he could do it, Lee kept a Negro mistress just like Thomas Jefferson and others were alleged to have done, but was better than old Tom at keeping it a secret.

Virginia and I were sympathetic to the slaves of the nineteenth century as well as to the Afro-Americans of the twenty-first century, who were their descendants.

The Blacks are human beings too, we contended, although like Lincoln, we knew Blacks were not our equals and that there was no need for them to vote or hold public office or anything like that. Lincoln also realized it was undesirable -- an abomination, he called it -- to mix the races, which God, in His wisdom, had made different, each with its own varied and distinct characteristics and abilities, strengths and weaknesses. Lincoln wanted to solve the race problem by deporting all the Negroes, slave or free, back to Africa where they came from. He explained all these views many times in his speeches, and especially in his famous debates with Stephen Douglas in 1858. In Wisconsin, people naturally have a good perspective on race, because they are not immersed in a Black Sea and can view racial issues objectively, from a distance. Anyway, we had no Black problem in Cross Plains Village, where there were only 19 head of Blacks, and those amounted to half of one per cent of the population. They didn't bother us and we didn't bother them. In truth, Blacks and Black questions never entered Virginia's or my head. Not for many years.

Anyway, back to our story. Virginia and I were delighted when the baby came, even if he was a month or so premature. Because of his early birth the hospital people decided it would be best to keep him in the neo-natal nursery for a few days for observation. Babies always look tiny, although at six pounds he was apparently doing extremely well for a premature infant, or "preemie," as they affectionately like to call them. His cranium was firm, the skull bones had already closed, his alertness, his movements, his hand grasp, and other measures of development, seemed remarkably advanced.

At first his outward appearance was like that of any other tiny baby there in the hospital. At first. Then after a few days his skin became darker. Especially around the ears. After five days he was the color of a young Comanche Indian, or a white person who had spent the winter at Vero Beach cultivating a gentle Florida suntan.

Suddenly concerned, I accosted the hospital authorities, worried whether the baby could have some dermatological disease or disorder causing a discoloration of his skin, or whether it was possible that it was what it appeared to be -- a Negro baby that they had mixed up in the nursery room. I had read that Negro babies are often born looking "white," but that their skin darkens in just a few days, perhaps on contact with oxygen or nitrogen.

"No" and "yes," said the hospital authorities: "No, there was no mix-up. Yes, it is a bi-racial baby." "Bi-racial" is the euphemistic term they used. Ugh. I had never heard it before.

"You mean a Mulatto? You mean Black, like a Darkie or a Negro?" I stammered as forcefully as I could, unconsciously using some terms I had learned as a child but which had fallen into obsolescence with the advent of the black power and civil rights movements of the sixties.

"Well, yes," came the gentle reply. "You can think of it as a genetic defect if you like, or simply a genetic difference. It is not so uncommon as you may think. Many of us carry black genes without even knowing it. Sometimes the influence of a distant ancestor suddenly manifests itself several generations later. It is occasionally called a throwback, or *tornatrás,* as they say in Mexico."

"That's impossible," I asserted in my rising anger and irritation. What are these people trying to do? "You must have mixed the cradles in the nursery," I declared in no uncertain terms.

"No way, Sir. There were no other births here that day, or within two days, fore and aft," he explained, sounding more like a sailor than a doctor.

"I don't believe you."

I went to a lawyer to get him to prepare a lawsuit. After three days of research costing me many bucks an hour, he concluded that it would be useless to pursue a legal case against the hospital. The medical records were convincing. That left me in a quandary. What to do?

My wife! That's it... that's where the answer lies.

My wrath and agitation were hitting the boiling point as I confronted her.

First I addressed her: "What were you doing when I was away in Copenhagen last summer?" She was all innocence and naïveté. She didn't know what I was talking about.

Then I accosted her: "Have you seen the baby? Have you had a good look at him in the last day or two? Your first-born son is turning into a little black tar-baby. Do you have Negro blood in your genteel veins from your Tidewater Virginia plantation ancestors?"

"No, of course I don't. Don't be ridiculous."

Finally I accused her: "All right then, tell me what you were doing when I was away in June and July last year!"

"What are you trying to imply?"

"I'm not implying anything. It's perfectly clear. I know what I'm saying. You were sleeping with someone else when I was away, weren't you? Got itchy and just couldn't wait until I got back. And you didn't even have the prudence or the decency or the discretion to pick a white man. You had to pick a Negro! a Nig! a Spade! a Coon, a Mulatto, a Darkie, a Jigaboo, an Ulotrichi, an Igbo! Or, as they call themselves now, a Black! Or was he just a Gentleman of Color?"

In my rage I seized her by the throat as the truth became clearer to me.

"No, I never..." she gasped. It was her last gasp.

* * * * *

I was gasping too, first from my exertion and then from the ghastly realization of what I had done. I was still inwardly seething, as you can understand. I had to go get a cold bottle of beer out of the refrigerator and try to cool myself down.

Now what to do? It is probably too late to apply artificial respiration. And I wasn't sure I would have wanted to do it anyway, certainly not if it meant putting my lips against the mouth of that... that creature. I was still furious, and also quite upset. I would rather die too than have my friends learn that my wife had given birth to a Negro. Or even a Mulatto. Spade. Tar Baby. Picaninny.

That was when I remembered my pistol. I had a .38 caliber Colt automatic that my father had rescued from the US Army when he was in the service. It took me an hour of frantic searching through drawers and closets and storage boxes everywhere before I found it. Then, there it was, in the bottom drawer of an old desk I only use to store stuff in, mostly pictures and seashells and a few old books with pressed maple leaves.

I picked up the gun, slid out the magazine, and opened the chamber. Empty. No bullets. I spent another half hour looking for the bullets without success. By then I was very tired and my head was aching. I started to go into the bedroom to lie down for a little rest, but saw something, or somebody -- some body -- there on the bed. Oh, my wife... So I went into the guest room and lay down there for about five minutes. But I couldn't rest, and certainly couldn't sleep. I wanted to die; that's what I wanted. I wanted to die, but didn't know how to do it.

The cops, they'll know. I thought of calling 911, but what good would that do now? I'll just go to the police station myself.

So I went on over to the Cross Plains police station on Brewery Road. It's just a converted double-wide trailer, and it looked closed. I knew the police chief slightly; I had met him once at a party, fellow by the name of Jeff Davis, if you can believe that. Nice guy, good beer drinker. Cross Plains Village has only about half a dozen on its police force, and two thirds of them are off duty at any given moment. Better I should go to Madison anyway. That's only twenty miles from here, or thirty minutes on a good day. They'll know what to do with me. I have heard that death by lethal injection can be relatively painless, especially if done correctly, and it's more reliable than shooting oneself. Sometimes, if you are lucky, they even hit the vein on the first stab, and nowadays they don't get their fluids mixed up as often as they used to.

After I got to the Madison police station it took another half hour before I could get anyone to hear my story. I had to take a number and await my turn. Finally I explained everything that had happened and they agreed to lock me up. The days and nights are muddy after that. I got a headache and a fever and an intestinal upset with palpitations. I remember going before a judge for a hearing or something. I don't think it was a regular trial; I was still living from day to day in my cell, semi-comatose, and not really concerned about my future or even aware of what was going on, knowing that I would die soon, one way or another.

Then one afternoon the guard said I had a visitor. It was my brother Eric. I haven't had much contact with Eric in recent years; he is four years younger than I am and a professor of sociology at the University of Chicago, in Chicago. Very liberal type, very bright; used to support the UN and Affirmative Action and that sort of thing, and even voted Democrat occasionally. And Eric is the one who was always most interested in family history, but paradoxically was never very interested in present-day family relationships. I hadn't seen him in four years, and haven't been getting much response to the Christmas cards I send him and his family occasionally.

"There's something you should know," he said. He had of course heard and read about Virginia's demise in the newspapers, although he had never tried to come and give me any sympathy until now.

"Yes, and what is that?" I offered, not showing much interest.

"It's something I should have told you a long time ago," he said, "but didn't, because I didn't want to upset you, knowing how you feel about Blacks and Lincoln and racial matters."

"All right, go ahead," I said with little enthusiasm.

"We have a Black ancestor."

"What! What are you talking about?" said I, beginning to wake up as a chill shot up my spine.

"It was in the Lee side of our family, 'way before the time of Robert E. Lee, who wasn't even a direct ancestor of ours. Incidentally, Lee was an octaroon himself; did you know that? Not many people do, because he could so easily pass for white. Ours was eleven generations ago," said Eric in his professorial tone of voice, "and it's extremely rare, but it does happen occasionally that a 'throwback' from so long ago will reappear, manifesting the outward and visible characteristics of the remote ancestor."

I was no longer hearing him, as he went on. I had a blinding headache by then and all I could see was red. Red and Black. *Rouge et Noir.* I could have written an epic novel if I had been able to write at all -- if I could have held a pen and lived long enough. Eric's final words brought me back to life, for the moment anyway.

"The baby is yours, Buck. You killed Virginia for nothing."

"Oh, shit" was on my tongue, but I couldn't get it out.

I was speechless.

THE END

Short Stories Encore

A Friend in Need

Opportunities don't always come knocking or your door. Sometimes you have to go out there and find them for yourself.

I was smart when I was in high school, usually top of my class academically, and I even played sports a little. I got into a few basketball games, although I am barely six feet tall. I was also on the second-string baseball team.

After I graduated, I could have gone to State College, where the tuition was very modest, but I was accepted at both of the Ivy League colleges I applied to, and that's where I wanted to go.

My parents and grandparents didn't have much money, being academics and educators themselves for the most part. (Curious, isn't it, how little most educators get paid and how costly most higher education is.) However, they agreed to pay my tuition and basic expenses if I agreed to work part-time to earn enough for my "incidentals" -- clothes, books, food, beer, dates, movies, any club fees, and of course toothpaste.

My Ivy League college had dropped ROTC as a protest during the Vietnam War, although MIT and other schools with less sensitive feelings for political science and human emotions kept it on. ROTC could have helped a lot with financial aid and scholarship money. Too bad.

217

I didn't like the idea of washing dishes at the Union cafeteria very much, so started looking for something else with more pay and fewer hours. About that time I just happened to pick up a Mensa Magazine belonging to my roommate and saw some advertisements from "sperm-banks" that were paying good money for donors with certain qualifications -- the right stuff -- like smart, white-skinned, healthy, and especially, smart. You know, high IQ. That sounded like me and that's what they wanted. Good.

So I immediately took the test and joined Mensa to prove I was smart, bought a hat and stayed out of the sun as often as I could to preserve my white skin, and got a flu-shot and some one-a-day vitamins to stay healthy.

Gathering all my qualifications together, I presented myself to the designated facility, sort of a clinic in a big building downtown on Madison Avenue, to begin work.

Well, that was just the beginning. The process of getting approved was rigorous. You wouldn't believe all the things they wanted to know, not just my Grandmother's middle name or the color of her eyes. I had to go back two or three times to give them all the information they wanted.

They wanted donors who were not just healthy, and white, and vigorous, but also good looking, with no obvious blemishes, and sperm that was also vigorous and could do remarkable things like swimming through hoops.

There were further restrictions on body types. If you were a man (it said, rather unnecessarily I thought) you must be at least six feet tall and physically fit, mesomorph body type (no ectomorphs or endomorphs please). Red-heads, and of course albinos, were not wanted, nor were applicants who were allergic to any foodstuffs, cat dander or sagebrush pollen. A big factor in my favor was my Danish grandmother -- God rest her soul. It seems that sperm banks love Danish sperm. Over one third of the ladies in the UK seeking sperm consistently choose something Danish if they can get it. But other hurdles still remained. The medical history form you had to fill out went on for eight pages. Things like:

No sex with a man from Africa since 1977

No drugs, now or ever

Sex only with a woman

No smoking

No history of fondness for alcohol beyond two ounces per day

No history of STD even if cured

No history of hereditary disease or deformities

Recent photograph of applicant

Baby photograph of applicant

Photographs of any known children of applicant

Record of every hospital admission, illness, disease, or operation, including tonsils, broken bones, and muscle strain or backache

All available medical records for every parent, sibling, aunt, uncle, cousin, and grandparent

Similar medical records for all children of siblings and other relatives, for the past three generations, preferably four

And then the sperm. I had to leave a sample so they could study them and make sure they had the Right Stuff and were the right size and had the right pH value and the right specific gravity and their tails were on the right end, and I don't know what all. They examined the sample with a microscope. The sperm had to be Olympic quality swimmers, know what direction to swim, have plenty of "motility" (whatever that is), have the right solvents in their noses for membrane-melting, and a good many other things only a PhD bio-chemist would understand.

So it's hard to imagine how anyone -- even an American with Danish ancestry -- could pass through all these barriers. Nevertheless I made it unscathed, although it would have been "nice," they said, if I had been a little more athletic in addition to my other high qualifications. So they accepted me and drew up an "arrangement" that looked like a global industrial development corporation contract. Initially I was to appear twice a week ready to go, Monday and Thursday afternoon, to make my donation, for which I was to receive $125 a visit. Not a bad deal for doing something I enjoyed and would probably be doing anyway.

"If you were in grad school we could give you $175 a shot; $175 each time you came here," the attendant said.

"I wouldn't think of coming anywhere else," I assured her. She also told me that PhD's normally get $200 per go, but they don't get many PhD donors because "by the time you get to be a PhD you are supposed to be making enough money that you don't have to consider supplicating your income in such a fashion." Those were her words. She seemed to regret the loss of all that good sperm and all those good genes. I had to agree and sympathize with her, telling her I too was sorry I was not a PhD. Her final instructions were no sex or alcohol for twenty-four hours before donation time. I didn't ponder the matter because I was not seriously contemplating any conflicting extracurricular activities at the moment, but I later realized that this restriction could be significant.

After a couple months of visits twice a week, they told me I was "popular" and that their clients liked my "profile." They wanted more. Accordingly they modified the arrangement: now I was to come three times a week, MWF at 4:00 pm. I liked the extra money and didn't think much about how the schedule could affect other possible conflicting extracurricular activities that might arise should the "time be right." Monday, Wednesday, and Friday evenings I would obviously be resting up a bit, and then Tuesday, Thursday, and Sunday evenings were out of bounds after 4:00 pm. because of the twenty-four-hour rule. That only left Saturday night. Oh well, so what.

And that's the way it stood for the next two years and that's the way it stands now.

The "Collections Room," where I went every time to make my donation, was a spotless ten-by-twelve cubicle with a cot, a chair, a desk with a TV, and some pictures and a stack of girly magazines. There was an adjoining bathroom with some jars, towels, tissues, and even a tiny shower stall. Everything one could dream of.

* * * * *

I guess it was the spring semester of my junior year that I met Rebecca. She was a student at our sister girls' college. I hadn't had much time or energy for girls in my college days up to then, but I suddenly found Rebecca cute, captivating, and compelling. With no plans or intentions whatsoever, we promptly fell in love. She was majoring in Anthropology but knew a lot about geography and sociology too. Also archeology. I found her fascinating and started seeing her when I could, supper sometimes, baseball games, occasional movies, long talks over evening coffee. I didn't really need to push the sex thing. Rebecca was more than a sex symbol or sex object anyway. She was a person too, and an interesting one at that.

It was only much later that I learned one of the reasons she liked me was that I didn't come on to her too fast -- that I didn't seem to "just want one thing," like so many of the other guys did. She thought I was being a gentleman out of respect for her and she admired me for that.

So things went on that way for quite a while. Finally she decided it was time to test the waters, or maybe she just got itchy, I'm not sure which. She suggested that she stay over with me in my dorm room one Saturday night when my roommate was away for the weekend trying his luck at Smith.

"Sure," I said, "why not?" although I usually try to use the weekends for resting up, after my MWF activities, or even do a little studying.

Saturday night I was ready to go to sleep when she cuddled up a little closer and asked, "Are you all right? Is anything wrong?"

"No, nothing's wrong," I said, "it's just... "

"Yes, just what?"

That was when I explained the whole thing to her; it had to come out sometime if I were going to go on seeing her. I told her all about my part-time job, how I made my spending money by being a sperm donor -- the whole bit.

"Oh, my!" she said, sounding somewhat surprised.

The next Monday at four o'clock I was back at the clinic as usual. I asked to speak to The Administrator for a minute. The clerks and secretaries and aides and managers there were all women as far as I could tell. You just have to get used to it. Anyway, there isn't much they haven't heard or seen at one time or another. The Administrator was a woman too, but I didn't let it bother me. I started in: "The pretty magazines and things in the collections room are rather old and familiar," I said. "I wonder whether we could bring in something else."

"Of course," she said. "I'm sorry you had to ask. I'm sure we can bring in some new magazines and pictures for Wednesday. Would you like anything else? A new video perhaps?"

"Well, not a new video, but there is something else."

"All right."

"I'd like to bring a friend."

"A friend?"

"Yes, a friend -- to help me."

THE END

Liberty or Death

Patrick Henry wasn't the only person to have the idea of liberty or death. We remember Henry because he expressed it so well -- and with spirit. But others have had spirit too -- or spirits. As anybody who has died and gone to Heaven knows, spirits are everywhere and can control our lives and our deaths in ways we are not aware of and perhaps cannot even imagine.

There are many types of spirits: there are alcoholic spirits (spirits who have an addiction to alcohol), Holy Spirits and Holy Ghosts, and as Henry would say, the Spirit of Seventy-Six. I had not been drinking at the time of this story and Henry had been dead for a number of years, so that left the Holy Spirit and the Voodoo Spirit for me to contend with, perhaps in combination.

*   *   *   *   *

It was August -- a good time to be out of New York City -- and I was in Rio de Janeiro for two weeks on a business trip. The company I work for imports Volkswagens made in Brazil for sale in the United States because they are cheaper than the ones made in Germany or the USA. I was supposed to investigate allegations that slave labor had gone into the manufacture of these vehicles. There had been reports circulating in left-wing American tabloids that as many as 50,000 slaves were still on active duty in Brazil. We did not want to touch anything made with slave labor of

225

course. I could not find any proof that our Brazilian suppliers were among the culprits -- those things are awfully hard to substantiate. My investigation didn't prove much either way. As they used to say in high school regarding the blue exam-book oath, anybody who would cheat would lie, and that may go for Big Business as well.

But I did learn something about the history of slavery in Brazil. It was so surprising that I was surprised we hadn't heard more about it back in school in New York, or why Lincoln and the Abolitionists didn't focus more of their attention South of the Equator. That's where the real action was, and where slavery was so much bigger and more frightful than anything we have ever known in South Carolina or even Alabama.

The total number of African slaves imported into Brazil had reached 4,000,000 by the time slavery was abolished there in 1888. This compares with various calculations of a total of between 288,000 and 300,000 slaves imported into the American colonies and the United States. Fortunately there were much higher survival rates and reproductive rates in the USA. In Brazil many died young and more were always needed. Incidentally, the number of slaves imported to the United States was only about half the number of people killed here in the Civil War, which was caused, at least partly, by the slavery question, although Lincoln denied that slavery was an issue. /1 Furthermore,

---

/1 In an open letter of August 22, 1862 to Horace Greeley, Lincoln wrote, in part, "My objective is not either to save or destroy slavery... if I could save the Union without freeing any slave I would do it."

there were thousands of indigenous natives like the Witoto and Papanases that had been enslaved in Brazil. Apparently these native South Americans were not well suited to slavery; they did not bear up well and died out rapidly in civilized captivity, thereby creating an even greater need for African slaves.

While I was in Rio I learned that the major Brazilian port for the entry and processing of African slaves was farther north, at the harbor of Salvador -- *São Salvador da Bahía de Todos os Santos* was its original name. Here incoming slaves were "processed" -- examined, washed, fed, checked for disease, exercised, and classified and labeled for sale and transport to various locations within the state of Bahía as well as other states throughout the land. Salvador de Bahía is the oldest city in Brazil; it was founded in 1549 (70 years before the Pilgrims came to Plymouth) and was the original colonial capital until 1763, when Rio became the capital. It subsequently grew rapidly, particularly in the twentieth century, and is now the nation's third largest city, after São Paulo and Río. I thought Salvador sounded like an interesting place.

One other thing: I like swimming and ocean beaches. It was winter down there and, although Rio temperatures were still relatively mild, the ocean water was pretty cold. Salvador was said to have the third best beach in the world and, being closer to the equator, should have ideal ocean temperature for swimming. Accordingly I planned a stopover in Salvador as a reward for my noble efforts on the job in Rio.

* * * * *

Upon arriving in Salvador de Bahía, I went straight to the Hotel Villa Bahía, an historic building in the historic Pelourinho district downtown. Stepping into the fusty lobby of that old hotel was like stepping into another world. Being one of the oldest hotels in the city, it had a certain shabby elegance. However, as it was rather run down and not directly on the beach, it was losing out to the big new all-inclusive resort hotels over on the oceanfront.

I immediately felt an eerie and musty silence as I came into the lobby, dark and cool though it was, with but a single clerk at Reception to check me in and give me my key. Nevertheless I was given a lovely large room on the ground floor, with high ceilings and tall windows protected from the street by heavy iron bars, as was normal. The usual furnishings, two chairs, tiny desk, chest of drawers, giant two-door *armoire*, and a smallish four-poster bed with canopy, and a pervasive viscid smell of antiquity and desuetude. There was only one picture on the wall, a framed lithograph of the Roman forum with its fragmented columns and a few caryatids that had lost their heads. A little out of place I thought at first, but maybe not. I unpacked my bag and lay down for a little rest.

When I awoke it was already getting dark -- I must have slept for two hours. I had to blink a couple of times to tell myself where I was. Oh yes, Salvador de Bahía. I was here to look around. I will start right here with the hotel.

Adjacent to the lobby was a large hall they called "El Salón." It had three great crystal chandeliers and five massive French windows on one side facing the plaza, but with heavy damask drapes three-quarters drawn. Along the

228

walls around the room there were numerous bookcases and shelves and display cases filled with artifacts and photographs. There were European and native carvings and statuary clustered in one corner, and portraits and framed historic drawings with old maps hanging on the walls. The place was a museum, reeking of history and decadence.

In the far corner near the servants' back entrance to the restaurant were two old mahogany tables cut down to serve as coffee tables, and several deep leather armchairs where one could enjoy a peaceful libation before the evening meal.

That was the physical layout. The spiritual layout was even more.

There was an incongruous mix of artifacts from Europe, Africa, and the Brazilian jungle. Dusty portraits and etchings of the Conquistadors, their sailing ships, and their armies. Outlines of the cramped interior layout of slave ships and drawings of African slaves chained together being marched from the river landings to their plantation homes. Paintings of slaves working on the sugar plantations and coffee plantations and diamond mines. And the Voodoo. People laugh at Voodoo, but let me tell you, Voodoo and Voodoo Mungo, the ubiquitous and omnipotent Voodoo God, are very real. There were two glass cabinets filled with Voodoo instruments and regalia -- Voodoo dolls, miniature Voodoo temples, talismans and fetishes with healing and rejuvenatory properties, Voodoo altars and images of Voodoo Gods and spirits, both male and female, carved with love and carved with spirit by special artisans who wielded the Hand of Mungo, the All Powerful. The hall seemed to vibrate with waves of voodoo spirits, penetrating everything in all directions.

Thinking about the past history of slavery in Brazil, I began to feel faint, almost overcome by the mysterious forces whose presence I sensed in the heavy atmosphere all about me. It was then that I first noticed two strange objects, one on each side of the great central French window. On one side there was the foot of an African elephant, about sixteen inches high, that had been preserved by a taxidermist and fitted with a large brass ashtray for a top. There were two black ribbons crossed over the ashtray suggesting that it was out of service.

By the other edge of the window, opposite the elephant foot, stood a life-size marble carving of the foot of a man. I felt a strange force pulling me toward the horrible looking little sculpture -- I had to examine it more closely. I was astonished by the remarkable skill of the artisan, and struck by the fine details of the muscles and skin texture, the bold relief of the tendons running to the toes, and even the precise form of the toenails and the protruding heel, a tell-tale characteristic of a black African. It was the foot of an African carved precisely in marble. Strange. Spooky.

Quite entranced, and hardly knowing what I was doing, I picked up the exquisitely macabre object, expecting it to be heavy, perhaps fifteen or twenty pounds, like any heavy piece of granite or marble that size. To my surprise I found it rather light, only three or four pounds at most. I looked more closely and concluded that the surface was coated with paint or whitewash. A shiver went up my spine and I put the object back down and shut my eyes to block out the sight of it and the image it evoked. With my eyes closed and my teeth clenched, I fell back into my easy chair and pressed my hands against my temples, feeling a little sick.

When I opened my eyes a moment later, there was a handsome middle-aged man, very black, sitting near me in one of the other comfortable leather chairs. I had not heard him come in. I don't know how long I had sat there with my eyes closed -- maybe longer than I realized. I should have been startled and perhaps even afraid upon suddenly confronting him, but I was not. It would have been more accurate to say I was in something of a daze. I touched my hands together and could hardly feel them. I raised my chin and looked at the man, but before I could say anything he preëmpted me.

"I see you are interested in Brazilian history and Brazilian slavery," he said gently, in slow Brazilian Portuguese so I could understand him.

"Why... why yes," I stammered, "I am enchanted by history."

"I could tell you something about the history of Bahía," he said. Still feeling almost in a trance myself, I told him I would like to hear it. So he started in:

"In the early eighteen hundreds we had some very prosperous land-holdings and plantations, or *fincas,* in the State of Bahía. 'La Bárbara' Plantation, not too far from here, was one of the most prosperous of all. At first it was the cultivation of sugar that made great fortunes for its

231

owners. At one time Brazil produced 75% of all the world's sugar. After sugar it was almost the same thing with coffee.

"Later the discovery and mining of diamonds brought more great wealth to the owners of La Bárbara Plantation. But the cultivation of sugar and coffee, and the mining of diamonds, were labor-intensive industries. The first Europeans to come to Brazil, the Conquistadors as they are sometimes called, needed help to exploit the riches of this land. They had no recourse but to make slaves of the native tribes living here, like the Witoto and the Papanases. Unfortunately, the Witoto and other native tribes didn't make very good slaves. They were too accustomed to their slothful, indigent way of life, and as slaves they died off at an alarming rate. That is when the European masters began to rely on the importation of African natives, who made much better slaves, were better workers, and had stronger constitutions and considerably longer life-expectancy. That went on for many years, even generations, bringing great prosperity to the masters of the estates, who were either European or, later, of mixed race.

"The early eighteen hundreds were a time of political upheaval. The Spanish and Portuguese colonies in the New World wanted to escape from the domination of their European overlords, and some of the slaves on the rich estates and plantations started to get ideas too -- they began to think they might like it better if they also were free. Some of them had heard about Haiti, which was the first country in the Americas in which Blacks were able to gain their freedom and take over control of the land.

"Now the slaves in our own La Bárbara Plantation, here in the state of Bahía, were well behaved, partly because they were from different parts of Africa. They were conflicted with ethnic tensions and dissension among themselves, because they belonged to tribes with different cultures and languages and did not understand one another. But the masters were nervous. In the last few years there had been various slave uprisings in other parts of Brazil, although never in La Bárbara.

"There was a slave named Olagantu who was quieter than the rest. He was also two or three inches taller than most of the others at La Bárbara, and he had the blackest skin of all.

"The master almost never heard him speak, but often saw Olagantu fixing his black-brown eyes on him with a brief but unblinking stare. The master knew a little about Voodoo and African spirits, and knew Olagantu was putting a hex on him. At first he tried to pretend it was only his imagination, but in his heart he knew it wasn't. It was real. He thereupon had trouble sleeping. He had headaches and indigestion. He had trouble with his wife. He realized Olagantu was plotting a revolt of the Blacks. He had a lot of money tied up in his slaves; slaves were valuable property. Losing even a few of them would be very costly. In his nervous and worried state he knew he had to do something. He could not let Olagantu continue to roam about the estate after working hours. He had no choice; he had to put a leg iron on Olagantu with a chain and a hundred-pound ball to restrict his movements and activities. Olagantu had to pick up the ball and carry it wherever he went, so he could not go very fast or very far.

233

"That relieved the Master's mind. Now, with Olagantu under control, he could relax and continue with his plans for increasing the profits of the Plantation. That went on quietly for a while.

"Then there was a big ruckus one night, or very early one morning before dawn. The county sheriff and other authorities were called in. They found to their horror that the Master had been murdered, his throat slit. There was a heavy trail of blood into, and out of, the Master's quarters, but it was not the Master's blood. A ball and chain were found outside the back kitchen door next to a bloody ax and a lump of something or other. The bloody abature led off into the woods. The officials were able to follow the trail for almost two miles until they came to a man sitting against a caoba tree with a smile on his face. It was Olagantu. He was dead. He had bled to death."

* * * * *

It was only with the greatest difficulty that I could open my mouth. "That's quite a story," I murmured.

"I must go," said the man as he stood up and started to leave. My eyes now clouded over as I looked at him. My whole body was shaking with goosebumps upon hearing this frightful tale. I then remembered the white foot by the window and turned to look at it, but it was no longer there. Gone. Disappeared. I know I had seen it and even touched it just a few minutes ago. I was sure I had. Then I turned back to the man as he was walking away. I blinked at what I saw and suddenly wet my pants, something I hardly ever do anymore. He was walking with a slight limp. I looked down and saw that he had a peg leg for a foot.

I blinked my eyes once more to clear the mist and looked at him again, but now he too was gone -- disappeared -- just as the white foot had disappeared.

THE END

Tell It to the Judge

"Tell it to the judge."

That's what he said, tell it to the judge. Those were his words. He was a big strong handsome cop. I am just a puny nobody. Although I am usually very polite, I am not terribly good-looking, and sometimes I don't make a very impressive impression. But this time I was right and he was wrong, whether or not anybody would believe it.

It all started on my way in to work a couple of months ago. I ride a little 49cc Honda motorbike because I can park it right in the basement of the office building where I work in downtown Washington. The big shots and top brass can park a limited number of automobiles there, but for us little shots and bottom brass there is also a parking area for a few bicycles and motorbikes, so that's why I have my Honda cycle. An engine of 49cc's isn't very powerful, and usually I have to go all out to keep up with the traffic. I can't even do that going up the Connecticut Avenue hill on my way home, where 25 MPH is about the maximum I can maintain. But it's very convenient transportation.

On my way in to work I usually take MacArthur Boulevard because there are no hills and I don't get screamed at for slowing up traffic. If I put my head down to reduce air resistance as much as possible, and give it full throttle like Barney Oldfield, I can slowly push it up to almost forty, just about the speed of the other vehicles in the right-hand lane. You don't want to get run down from behind on a little Honda bike.

So there I was, coming in to work the other day, with my briefcase strapped on behind me, doing the best I could in the middle of Washington's rush-hour traffic, when the surprise came. The surprise was a blaze of flashing red and blue lights on one of the cars flowing past me on the left lane, but this one car had slowed to an even speed with me and its driver was gesticulating for me to pull over. I pondered what to do for about a nano-second then eased to the side and stopped. Now we would block traffic; too bad. Perhaps I have a low rear tire that is slowing me down, that the nice policeman wants to tell me about.

No, that wasn't it. The reason the nice policeman pulled me over was to ask me a question. I don't usually mind if people ask me questions. They do it at work all the time. But what this fellow wanted to know was whether I knew what the speed limit on MacArthur Boulevard was at that time of the morning. As he was apparently an Officer of the Law I thought he would have known about such things without having to ask. Nevertheless, I politely smiled and told him I thought it was probably thirty-five miles per hour. As it rapidly dawned upon me that his question was probably more rhetorical than information-seeking, I thoughtfully added, "Why, how fast was I going?"

"I wasn't able to clock you," he said, sounding somewhat frustrated upon confessing his incomplete knowledge, "but you must have been doing at least forty or forty-five."

Although I was still somewhat nervous after riding several blocks with a giant Mercedes Benz sedan pressuring me ten feet behind my rear fender, I righteously explained that I was calling upon all 49cc's of my machine to help me keep up with the traffic and avoid impeding the flow of cars or risk getting run down myself. To make it even easier for the fellow to get the picture, I pointed out that I had been riding in the slower right-hand lane, the safer one for me. I added, apparently without effect as it turned out, that a stream of cars on my left were flowing past me with aplomb.

I guess the officer either did not like what I had to say, or else found it so interesting that he wanted to share it, for his surprising response was a snappy, "Tell it to the judge." In fact, I believe those were his exact words. It crossed my mind that he might have thought my explanation so fascinating that he believed his friend the judge would find it equally engaging. Those fellows must lead an uninteresting life among the gasoline fumes and dusty air of the inner city, so you can see why they need an occasional chuckle to lighten their day.

However, his countenance bore an expression that belied his readiness to view any matter with amusement that morning, regardless of its innate hilarity. Therefore, surmising that he was not in a jocular mood, I wiped away my own smile, which I habitually keep in ready reserve for use in awkward situations, and sought out his eye, saying into it quite politely and very seriously indeed, "Yes, Sir! I will Sir! Certainly Sir!" My accommodating response did not seem to cheer him up very much, but nevertheless he scribbled something on a piece of blue paper. He shoved it

239

into my window and announced, "Here." Subsequent examination revealed that the blue paper was an invitation to meet with his friend the judge some three weeks hence, conveniently giving me the precise time and place for said rendezvous.

* * * * *

I duly arrived at the designated time and place to meet the judge, a fellow of indeterminate ancestry, pushing middle age. I was sad to see that he bore a permanent frown deeply engraved upon the countenance he was presenting to the public that day. That sometimes happens when one's wife has not been nice to one, or one's morning coffee is too hot. As is the case for many other things as well, there is an ideal temperature for wives and coffee. Medium warm, I would say. A pity, I thought, that anyone had to start his day with something so unpleasant on his mind as to make him seem that sullen and indisposed.

The aforementioned officer of the law was also present, now radiating overweening confidence and satisfaction as he contemplated the outcome of today's session facing me in court, a scenario he knew so well.

"What do we have here?" said the judge with a dismissive tone to his voice, addressing the burly policeman and coming directly to the point.

With the assurance of a Panzer tank commander demolishing an outhouse in the Libyan desert, the nice policeman irrefragably offered a blatant imposture in his

240

booming baritone voice, "Your honor, I clocked this man coming in on MacArthur Boulevard at fifty miles an hour in a thirty-five mile zone."

The judge, in no humor to be humored, and probably annoyed to have been awakened so early for such a trivial case, swiveled over in my direction with a frown that told me he had already closed his mind: "And what do YOU have to say for yourself?"

I had memorized my defense story word for word, how I would explain the truth in detail, but my preparation was to no avail. I could say nothing -- I was thoroughly and utterly nonplussed.

Speechless.

THE END

Always True

Herman was not a tiger in the bedroom, but he had other redeeming qualities, as we shall see.

He was a nice guy. A decent fellow. He had come from a fine old Virginia family and had been well brought up. He was quiet and easygoing; he was tidy and liked to do things properly. In school he persevered in what he did, but he was never either a brilliant student or an outstanding athlete. He got mostly "C's" with an occasional "B" or "D". He even got an "A" once. He went out for football, and got on the squad as a defensive guard, but didn't actually get into a varsity game until late in the season of his senior year when they were beating Eastern High 41-7 in the fourth quarter. But he never missed a practice or a scrimmage, and at game time he always cheered his teammates on in good humor.

In addition to his unrequited interest in football, Herman loved cars and, especially, trucks. His uncle owned a farm in the next county, and as a teenager Herman used to visit his uncle on weekends. As soon as Herman was old enough, the overseer would let him drive the farm trucks and tractor -- on weekends when there was no football game, of course.

Herman had to study hard for his schoolwork though, which did not come easily to him, and in June, 1967, a month before his twenty-first birthday, he graduated in the

243

top half of the bottom quarter of his high school class. With the Vietnam War in full swing, Herman, and many of his classmates, enlisted in the Army rather than waiting to be drafted, because that gave them some choice regarding their assignment, that they would not have had otherwise.

Herman was fascinated by the powerful trucks and combat vehicles he saw in the Army and knew right away what he wanted to do. He volunteered for the Army Transportation Corps, was happily accepted, and went through training at Fort Benning Georgia, Fort Bragg North Carolina, and an assignment at the Letterkenny Arsenal in southern Pennsylvania.

Over the next few years, Herman served two tours of duty in Vietnam, duly rising to PFC and finally to Corporal. His work consisted mostly in driving supply trucks between the ocean front at Cam Ranh Bay and the adjacent air strip, but also helping in first echelon motor vehicle maintenance. He was happy in his work, and was able to save most of his pay, including a 25% bonus for hazardous duty.

After the end of the Vietnam war, many of Herman's Army friends were leaving the service and going back to civilian life. Herman also considered that briefly, but it didn't take him long to realize he was happy doing what he had been doing in the Army, and he decided to stay in for a while and at least see what future assignment the Army might have in store for him. As a "reward" for his solid service in Vietnam, the Army then sent Herman to Germany, where he was assigned transport duties, which consisted mostly in hauling supplies and equipment from one US Army base to another. He had a definite route and schedule which he liked fine, and he could not understand why some of his Army colleagues complained about the rigid unvarying routine and the boredom of repeatedly traveling the same old routes with the same old schedules. Herman never saw anything to complain about. He liked his trucks, he liked his work, and he was comfortable in his routine.

Before he went into the Army, Herman had never had many dates and had never developed any special interest or relationship with a girl -- or young woman, as they were beginning to prefer to be called. He wasn't homosexual or anything like that, but just a little slower to progress in that direction than most young men his age. When he got to Vietnam, he was shocked at the aplomb with which American soldiers, and even officers, took up with the Vietnamese women and began carrying on and cohabiting, and fraternizing and fornicating, and I don't know what all. His distaste for the crude, demotic romances he saw going on around him was mitigated only by the fact that he personally did not feel attracted to oriental women. He would acknowledge, however, that the Vietnamese ladies did have a certain grace and even elegance as they drifted about in their ubiquitous Ao Đai (pronounced "Ow Yai,") dresses worn over the traditional white satin pyjama slacks. The Ao Đai is a tubular sheath that is standard feminine attire in Vietnam, having been developed for the stick-like form of the typical thin, willowy oriental body. To Herman they looked like china dolls, and about as warm.

However, in Germany it was a different story. In Germany Herman found himself surrounded by attractive and interesting women on every hand. Of course, he had to be rather cautious, particularly at first, because he didn't know much about any of them -- about their backgrounds that is -- who their parents and forebears were, how they had been brought up, or what schooling they had received. Accordingly, the first German woman he had a date with was a clerk named Ursula, who worked at the same US Army base. Although she was not the most beautiful woman in the world, she wasn't bad looking either. She must have gone through a certain vetting process to get her present job. She had a gentle, sweet nature; she apparently bathed reasonably often, dressed conservatively, and spoke softly; consequently she did not frighten Herman away, as did some of the flashier, faster, Fräuleins. When Herman worked up the courage to ask her out to dinner one day, she delighted him by accepting the invitation. Herman was further pleased to learn that Ursula's father also was working for the Americans, at another base nearby, so he also must have been checked out along the way. Herman made a point of meeting him, and Ursula's mother as well, at the first opportunity. Although the encounters were rather formal and cool, Herman considered them satisfactory. They made everything Proper and All Right.

Herman saw as much as he could of Ursula for the rest of his three-year assignment in Germany. As he was now 34 years old, with no other prospects or particular domestic interests on the horizon, he realized that he was unlikely ever to find a better wife than Ursula. He also acknowledged that there might be the basis for some true love stirring in his heart for her. So, to the surprise of no one who knew them, he asked her to come with him to the United States and marry him. She accepted, looking forward to an exciting new life in Amerika.

Herman had grown up in Arlington, Virginia, and his parents, who stemmed from the FFV, /1 still lived there. Accordingly, after his tour in Germany, he was delighted to be assigned to an Army post at Aberdeen, outside of Baltimore, Maryland, known as the Proving Ground. It was just a two-hour drive from his parents' house on a good day. The couple had a proper wedding at St. John's Church in old Alexandria, took a week-long honeymoon to Niagara Falls, and then went to Aberdeen to report for duty.

Herman was always proud of his new wife -- he enjoyed showing her off to his mother and his friends in Arlington and, later, to his Army buddies and co-workers on the job. She accepted his adulation with tolerance and a smile.

By then Herman had 14 years of military service and had been promoted to Sergeant. He and his bride slipped easily into a comfortable life at Aberdeen Proving Ground, living in Army housing, in a small but adequate duplex right on the base. Ursula, already knowing something of Army life and organization, was able to find her way around easily and comfortably. She knew the routine of the Commissary, the PX, and other facilities, from her work with the US Army in Germany. Herman was now eligible for the NCO Club, which became their base for social activities and a means for Ursula to develop friendships with other Army wives.

/1 FFV (First Families of Virginia), an historical association for descendants of adventurers that weren't able to wait for the Mayflower. They settled in the area of Jamestown, Virginia in 1607. Actually some of the FFV people were quite nice.

Herman loved his work. He viewed himself as being rather like a doctor in a hospital devoted to saving human lives, but he was saving truck lives. He had special names for his favorite trucks, like Dolly, and Buster, and Constantine. His boss said Constantine needed a whole new engine, the old one was hopeless. "The engine is her heart," said Herman, "let me fix it. It will take some work, but I know I can do it." He was emotionally and wholeheartedly attached to his job. It was his life.

"Impossible," said the Captain. "You'll be wasting your time."

But it was a challenge for Herman. He went back to the shop after dinner a few times to work on Constantine in the evening. He soon realized that the job was going to be more than he had estimated, but now he couldn't admit that he was wrong. Some people might call Herman hard-headed; he was certainly resolute and determined, even doggèd and tenacious. He had his pride. He would save more of his evenings to work on that truck's engine in his own time, Constantine's engine. He had to take the engine all apart, pull off the head, take out the pistons, re-bore the cylinders, fashion new pistons, rods, and bearings, turn the crankshaft, fit oversize rings, grind the valves, and even weld a crack in the engine mount itself, the whole bit. He was a determined fellow.

Ursula found their married life, well... satisfactory... especially at first, when Herman would save two nights a week just for her. But he was not a tiger in the bedroom. She still remembered the night -- was it their wedding night? -- when she had taken a shower and tried to slip quietly from the bathroom straight into bed. But he saw her coming out of the bathroom and was surprised. He thereupon surprised her even more, saying, "Darling, you're naked! Here, put something on," throwing her his own pyjama top.

Her best friends of course were other young Army wives. In her little group there were four or five Americans, two Germans, one French, one Dutch, an Australian, even one from Ireland, and sometimes a few others. The two German ladies, Ingrid and Brita, were, not surprisingly, her best friends, especially Brita. They met frequently for coffee or tea or tennis and occasional meals with their husbands, but usually it was just women. That way they could talk about anything.

They talked about their life on the base, about shopping and clothes, about their children, about their own childhood in the old country, and about any part-time jobs that were available. In due course their topic of conversation naturally came around to men, a subject about which they all had something to say. They could talk with aplomb about their husbands, about their first time with a man, about their old boyfriends, and, in the case of Monique, the French woman, about her *new* boyfriend. At first the young ladies spoke of their husbands. "My husband is short, but he is wonderful," said the Australian.

"Yes. Size isn't everything," said Mika, the Dutch girl. "It's what you do with what you have."

"I only meant that he is not very tall, but at least he is a few centimeters taller than I am."

"That's nice. Every centimeter... I mean every inch a man. That helps, as long as he doesn't hurt you."

Then, when there came a lull in the conversation, Monique spoke up: "I have a confession to make, but you must promise not to tell anyone."

"Oh, we'll never tell," said several ladies almost in unison.

At first, Ursula was shocked, but fascinated, and Brita politely feigned nonchalance, as Monique, a married woman, proceeded to talk of having a boyfriend. It was a romance outside the family, with a man she was not married to, or even related to. Monique said his name was Peter and added he was well named, although it took some of the others a while to catch that one.

Trudy insisted her Californian husband was the most active thing on two legs, and she could not imagine having two men in her life. As she explained it, her one husband often tired her out so much that she had to go back to bed for a two-hour morning map. "Maybe you don't give your husband enough attention," she would tell Monique.

"Oh, yes I do -- I used to try every night, but once a week seems to be his limit. The other nights we just watch TV, although sometimes he holds my hand while we are sitting on the couch together."

"How sweet."

"I was only 19 when I had my first boyfriend, and I will never forget him," said one of the ladies.

"Nineteen?" said another. "That's almost an old woman. What took you so long? I was 16," she added with a touch of pride in her voice.

"Were you precocious or just lucky?"

"Neither, actually. And I will admit that it wasn't very good -- the first time, that is. He didn't know what he was doing, and of course I didn't either, but at least I had some instincts."

"I agree. Good romance is founded on good instincts. Look at a pair of fruit flies or mourning doves. How do you think *they* learn about romance...? from Audubon paintings?"

"Yes, but sometimes it's nice if the man is a little older and knows something."

"You mean older and wiser. The 'wiser' is the most important part."

"Well yes, I guess so. It does help if he knows what he is doing."

"I always like to teach them, myself. It's rather fun to show them how."

"You keep saying 'them'; have you had multiple lovers?" said Trudy, trying to put a gently shocked tone to

251

her voice. "I've always been faithful to *my* husband; he's enough for me. Too much, sometimes."

"I never had more than one at a time -- I wouldn't do *that*."

"I don't know what difference it makes whether you had them all at one time or four different times."

"If you had them all at once, you would only have to go to confession once," said the Irish girl. "Otherwise you would have to go four times."

"Don't be sacrilegious."

"I was only kidding."

"Four times? You mean you've had four boyfriends?"

"Four that I can remember."

"Men can be quite exciting. I look at other men too sometimes, although I know my husband would never look at another woman."

"Don't bet on it."

"I wish *my* husband *would* look at some other women more often," said Trudy.

"My husband only looks at me once or twice a month," said Ursula.

252

"Do you mean...?" said Rose.

"Yes, that's what I mean."

"You poor thing," said Mary.

"Maybe you are lucky," said Trudy. "My husband looks at me three or four times a night, and even more on weekends. That is, unless there is a football game on TV. Sometimes I wish they had football every night. All night. And I could get some rest."

"Wasn't there a book called "Once a Week Is Not Enough"? said one of the women.

"No, I think it was just "Once Is Not Enough," said another.

"Does that mean what I think it means?"

"Maybe she was talking about chocolate. You know, one piece is not enough."

"Could be. You can chew on chocolate drops before you swallow them, but then you always want another. Chocolate bars last longer if you just suck them."

"I don't think that's what she meant at all."

"All right, go read it then."

"What's your boyfriend like?" Rose asked Monique, changing the subject -- sort of.

253

"He's an officer, a Second Lieutenant. He just graduated from West Point last year. He's long and he is tall, and he is... well... great. And he isn't even married," added Monique as an afterthought.

"If I were going to take a lover, I think it would be wiser to go off base. Find a Greyhound Bus driver or get an American Airlines pilot over at BWI Airport."

"You get them where you find them. I found one once, but he was no better than my husband. And he gave me the itch. So I went back to my husband. I mean, full time. It wasn't as though I had ever really left him."

"All this talk is making me horny," blurted out Ursula, surprising herself and turning quite red.

"Well, don't look at me," said Marilyn, "I can't help you in that department; there's nothing queer about me, about me, about me."

"Except your hairdo," said someone.

"Go back to your husband," said Rose. "He'll be home in a couple of hours, when he gets off work.

"This is only Tuesday," said Ursula.

"So it's Tuesday. So what?"

"We're not scheduled until Saturday. Herman likes to pace himself."

"Oh, Good Grief! You poor thing."

All this talk about how great their husbands were, and about how great their boyfriends were, was upsetting to Ursula. In talking to the girls, she was embarrassed by her limited experience with men. She had known only one man -- her Herman -- and had little to brag about. Her ego was suffering up against these sophisticated women. Maybe she had been missing something. Maybe she needed a new light to brighten up her life -- something or someone she could brag about to the girls. She needed to prove her femininity, her charm, her sensuality, and fulfill her untapped -- or only slightly tapped -- potential.

Of all the energetic men the ladies had been talking about, Peter, the Second Lieutenant from West Point, sounded most interesting, appealing, and desirable, thought Ursula. He might do very nicely, both to satisfy her own inner craving and to give her something to brag about to the others. And furthermore, it would mean she wouldn't have to keep pestering her husband so much. Yes, her goal should be to captivate this fellow, this new, clean-cut, young West Point graduate, Monique's boyfriend. "The French Woman's Lieutenant," was the expression that came to her as she visualized him in her mind's eye with a chuckle at her cleverness. /2

So she did it. And he was great. Just as Monique had said. They set up a regular routine. On those evenings

---

/2 with apologies to John Fowles, author of
The French Lieutenant's Woman

when Herman went to work on Clementine and his other trucks, Ursula and the young Lieutenant went to work too.

The Lieutenant brought some lively new excitement into Ursula's life. He sensibly offered no objection to her suggestion that it would be better not to risk upsetting Herman by telling him of the arrangement, or burden his mind by bringing him up to date on their activities. They had their own little "don't ask don't tell" policy, and it worked out fine. That went on for four months.

Then, surprisingly, the stalwart Lieutenant suddenly insulted Ursula by marrying his childhood sweetheart, who lived just a few miles away in Bel Air, Maryland. To make matters worse, he added injury to insult, telling Ursula they had to end their affair. Ursula protested bravely -- she had gotten used to the arrangement. Peter was warm, comfortable, and fulfilling, as it were. She didn't want to give him up just because he had gotten married, and told him so. But no dice. He suddenly was all "duty, honor, country," and he wouldn't listen. He told her to go back home to her husband or find someone else, advice that Ursula didn't need.

But the Lieutenant had helped to develop and ripen the potential of Ursula's instincts and talents more fully, and she had become a warm, ripe, active woman, hitting on all fours. So she took his advice anyway and did find someone else. A Captain this time. And although he was already married, he was very good. Very experienced.

All this time Ursula was also careful to attend to her husband and all his needs, meager as some of them were.

At the same time she would occasionally say, "I think you are in love with your trucks."

He would never argue the point, but would only half-jokingly reply, "Maybe I am, but I love you too." Herman was delighted that his wife always seemed happy. "You are the only one I have ever really loved, you know."

"Really loved, indeed... That's nice," thought Ursula.

They gave the world the appearance of a happy married couple. And it's true, that's what they were. A happy married couple that lived in Middle America, even if he did look closely at her only once a month. Well, sometimes twice a month. They were happy.

Ursula eased any nascent qualms of conscience caused by her wayward behavior by more assiduously than ever attending to her husband's every desire and whim. She cooked gourmet meals for him, pressed his pyjamas and undershirts the way he liked them, listened with rapt attention and sympathy when he told her about the trucks he had taken apart and was trying to put together. She turned down his side of the bed for him, and always made sure there was a clean glass of cold water and a roll of Tums on his bedside table should he want anything during the night. She loved Herman, very much -- in her way. Or his way. She happily cared for him with a perennially good nature nourished on the satisfaction she enjoyed from her well-rounded, active life. Herman loved her dearly; he often told her he was happy that she was happy. She sweetly thanked him for that. She was happy that he was happy that she was happy. He had everything he could ever want in a wife, and he told her so. She let that one go by.

This pleasant situation lasted four years, until Herman got a new assignment, but Ursula had learned how to be happy, and how to keep her husband happy, without burdening him with details of her life that might be embarrassing. In the years to come, she was able to work out similar arrangements wherever they lived.

Throughout the next fifty years, Ursula and Herman maintained a genteel home life, overtly proper and satisfactory. Herman had retired after 37 years service, having attained the rank of Master Sergeant, about as high as an enlisted man could go short of Warrant Officer. After retirement he started his own little truck-repair business, not to make money, but "for fun," as he put it.

Ursula was an ideal wife: she kept herself pretty, still bathed fairly regularly, did the laundry and changed the sheets once a week whether they needed it or not. She was pleasant to Herman's truck-loving friends, and fed them generously when he sometimes brought them home for supper. She always made sure there was plenty of Bud Lite, beans, and hotdogs in the fridge.

The life of Herman and Ursula together was indeed satisfactory -- as far as it went. The two did care for each other, and were content with things as they were. Neither had any urge or intention of rocking the boat; Herman rounded out his life with his devotion to trucks, first as his job and later as his consuming avocation, while Ursula continued to fill her needs by means of a number of other

258

lovers, maybe two or three dozen. One lasted almost twelve years; others six months or a year or two. But in no way did Ursula neglect he dear husband. He was everything else to her a loving husband could be, and every month he still saved one or two nights solely for her.

She was content with her life and was comfortable knowing that her dear Herman was comfortable too; she showed him she loved him by cooking his food and taking care of the household, and by contributing to the family finances from her various part-time jobs through the years. Although he told her all about his trucks, she never found it necessary to mention her extra-curricular affairs, which had become a basic part of her life -- a necessary part, given her husband's limited romantic inclinations. As far as he knew, or as far as he was concerned, her romantic inclinations corresponded precisely to his. The two of them were ideally compatible. He could not imagine that she would ever look at another man, but in truth he never gave it a thought.

And that's the way it was. She was happy with him and loved him for what he was, although he was not a person who ever could have fulfilled all her needs.

He was happy with her because she *did* fill all *his* needs, and because she wasn't too demanding.

Then he died.

But on his deathbed, his last words were, "Darling... "

"Yes, my Dear."

"There's something I want to tell you."

"Yes, my Dear."

"I have always loved you," he said feebly, but with a quiet note of pride in his own righteousness and the good life he had given her.

"Yes, my Dear."

"I want you to know... "

"Yes, my Dear."

"I have never been unfaithful to you."

"*No shit*," she thought.

But she held her tongue and simply gave him a tender kiss on the forehead.

"Yes, my Dear."

A gentle smile crept over his countenance as he closed his eyes for the last time.

THE END

A Civil War Story

Usually it is best for husbands to follow the advice of their wives, and do what we tell them to do. Usually.

Although some great women did quite well on their own and got rather famous; others worked through their husbands. Women like Joan of Arc, and Queen Victoria, and Shirley Temple Black, and Betsy Ross of course, were more famous than any husbands or boyfriends they might have had along the way. Other women have made their mark or influence in world affairs by working through their husbands, pushing them around and telling them what to do, especially when necessary to do so. Some such women who come to mind include Edith Wilson and Eleanor Roosevelt, who nursed their husbands and ran the White House while they were recovering from strokes or polio or something. Also Dolley Madison, and Claire Boothe Luce, and the Soong sisters, one of whom was married to Sun Yat Sen and the other married to Chiang Kai-shek, to name a few.

One influential wife we don't hear much about was Mary Jane Kingsley Buckner, the wife of Civil War General Simón Bolívar Buckner. Simón Buckner, born in 1823, was possibly named for the well-known South American Revolutionary Hero born in Caracas in 1783, exactly forty years earlier. That famous gentleman was known to most of his acquaintances by his nickname, Simón Bolívar, although his real name was Simón José

261

Antonio de la Trinidad Bolívar y Palacio Ponto y Blanco. It is unclear why the parents of our Civil War general gave their son only a portion of the original Simón's full name, but few history books have deemed the matter of sufficient importance to be pursued.

Simón Bolívar Buckner, unlike his namesake, had no comprehensive plan for the future of the world or even for his own nation. Like many in his conflicted generation, especially people living in Kentucky, Buckner was unsure which side to favor when the split occurred in the United States leading to the frightful Civil War, where more people were killed than in all of our other wars combined, from the Revolutionary War to our wars in Iraq and Afghanistan, incouding WWI, WWII, Korea, Vietnam plus a number of others.

Buckner was born in Munfordville, a town near Mammoth Cave in central Kentucky with a population of 250 that has since grown to almost 1,500. He grew up preferring to be called simply "Bolivar" or "Bo." His father, Aylett Hartswell Buckner, was born in Albemarle, Virginia and came to Kentucky with his parents when he was twelve years old. Bolivar's mother, Elizabeth Ann Morehead, was also born in Virginia, to a prominent family of Warrenton, and like her husband-to-be also came to Kentucky as a child. So "Bo" had definite Southern connections and background. Munfordville is but a short distance from Fort Henry and Fort Donelson to the south, across the border in Tennessee, both of which were destined to become famous, or infamous, in their own right, as soon as the war had gotten up some momentum. Jefferson Davis, like Abraham Lincoln, was also born in that area, about a hundred miles to the west.

Bolivar's father, Aylett Buckner, had served in the Army as a youth during the War of 1812, but chose not to follow the military as a career; he liked the prosperous life of a gentleman farmer -- "planter" was the term he preferred. But he knew enough about war to tell his son Bolivar something about it and stimulate his interest.

Young Bolivar was quite bright for his size; he craved knowledge and education, and took full advantage of his father's extensive library and the opportunities for learning offered by the best schools in the area. By the time he was seventeen he was well prepared to go on to further studies. By chance he learned that a previous acquaintance of his, a slightly older lad named Charles McLean, of nearby Muhlenberg, had just dropped out of West Point. Bolivar rushed to his Congressman and was able to secure the replacement appointment, and duly entered as a Cadet in the spring of 1840.

Bolivar liked the Academy and also New York. He graduated eleventh in his class in 1844, and was promptly sent to Sackett Harbor, New York, for garrison duty on the shores of Lake Ontario. It was at Sackett Harbor that he met and befriended a young teeny-bopper named Mary Jane, the daughter of an Army Major serving at the post, Julius Kingsley. Mary Jane was too young for anything to happen between them beyond a mutual admiration, so the breakup caused by Bolivar's reassignment the following year was not too onerous. Bolivar was assigned back to

263

West Point, this time as an Instructor in History, Geography, and Ethics. He hadn't forgotten the lovely little waif from the lake shore, and was delighted to learn shortly thereafter that her father was returning with his family to his home in Waterbury, Connecticut, about seventy miles from West Point, near enough for occasional visits. Mary Jane was now fourteen going on sixteen, and definitely rounding out into something worth looking at. Then suddenly the Mexican War loomed on the horizon.

After just one year's teaching at West Point, Bolivar felt his duty called him to join General Winfield Scott's planned invasion of Mexico while the opportunity to gain battle experience was ripe. So that's what he did. He fought commendably in several battles there, from Veracruz to Chapultepec. It so happened that his best friend and buddy in service in Mexico was Lt. Ulysses S. Grant. The two had known each other at the Point, where Grant was just one year ahead of Buckner. Now, in Mexico, the two not only fought side by side, but, after the fighting essentially ended in September 1857 with the Battle of Chapultepec, they stayed on in Mexico for several months, until the formal peace treaty was signed in February1848 giving half of Mexico to the United States as a reward for our valiant belligerent efforts. The two young men, with practically no garrison duties or responsibilities of significance to restrain them, were able to roam about the Mexican countryside for the next four or five months, checking out the *vino*, *señoritas*, and *canciones*. They even undertook a mountain-climbing expedition up the steep slopes of Mount Popocatepetl, quite an endeavor in those days, with no modern climbing equipment, axes or pitons, plastic tents or oxygen gear. Popocatepetl was, and is, a 17,500-foot volcano, the second highest mountain in North America and more than 3,000 feet higher than the great Mount Whitney in California. /1

The expedition was only partly successful. Simon made it to the top and duly planted an Iwo-Jima-type flag on the rim of the volcano, but Ulysses was unable to share in this accomplishment, having dropped out at 12,000 feet, apparently out of breath or out of tequila -- we are not sure which, possibly both. They rejoined in time to see a few more sights and pick up some sarapes and onyx ash trays and letter openers to take back to the States as presents and souvenirs when the time came to depart the following spring. The two did not see each other for a while after that, but they did remember their happy times together.

Although Grant and Buckner came from different strata of society, their lives continued to follow certain parallels. Both were married within a year or two after their return from the Mexican War. Both had assignments of little significance in the West in the early 1850's, and both got bored with Army life and resigned their commissions in 1854 or 1855, whether asked to do so or not. Both went to work with family businesses for the next few years.

/1 In 1910 Buckner revisited Mexico, this time with his son, Simon Bolivar Buckner Jr., a recent graduate of West Point himself, who repeated his father's feat of scaling Mt. Popocatepetl. Simon Jr. subsequently rose to become a three-star General, and he lead the US 10th Army invasion of Okinawa. He was hit by shell fragments and died in June 1945. He was our highest ranking officer killed in WWII.

Buckner did well helping manage the Kingsley family's expanding real estate operations in Chicago after his father-in-law died leaving Mary Jane with a large interest in the business. By then Buckner had settled in Louisville, where he and his wife began to live life in comfort in genteel society with people of their own class. He maintained the rank of Colonel in the State Militia, mostly an honorary title, in addition to his position as CEO of the family real estate development corporation. He had a loving wife and life was smiling upon him.

Buckner's wife, Mary Jane Kingsley, was a sedate Puritan brunette who was born and raised in Waterbury, Connecticut, not too far from West Point. She was the daughter of Major Julius Kingsley, also a West Point graduate, class of 1823, so she knew something of military life. She was a lovely, likeable girl who was well brought up, went to the proper schools for young ladies, and as a teen-ager charmed Connecticut society with her sweet smile and graceful manner. Her two best friends in school had been a delightful pair of sisters from a fine old Norfolk, Virginia family, young ladies Mary Jane stayed in touch with all her life. The two "could not believe" that Mary Jane, "being so nice," was not also a Southern Girl who had gone "out north" to get an education. "She is so nice," they used to say, "if she is from Connecticut, she must be from *Southern* Connecticut." Smiles.

When still a pre-teen with big blue eyes, Mary Jane met young Lt. Buckner one summer at Sackett Harbor where her father was stationed for garrison duty. She never forgot her first impression of the young West Pointer, and, a few years later, when the opportunity presented itself and she was nubile and ripe enough, she fell completely in love with the handsome young officer, who was only nine years her senior -- a nice balance. He had recently returned from heroic service in Mexico, which only added to his charm. They were married in the spring of 1850 at her aunt's estate in Old Lyme, Connecticut, where important things like weddings were handled properly. Mary Jane was looking forward to getting out of stuffy Connecticut and moving to Louisville where there was more fresh air and whence she might see the Illinois side of her family occasionally.

But she really loved her dear Simon Bolivar. It is true that she liked to boss him around a bit when she had the chance, but she would willingly follow him when the Army sent him hither and yon on various assignments, regardless of whether she was supposed to or not. Officers' wives frequently accompanied their husbands to military posts; Grant's wife, Julia Dent, did too. Mary Jane often saw wounded and crippled soldiers, residue from the Mexican War, sometimes without arms or legs, and her heart went out to them. She volunteered to help at various Army hospitals, where casualties from the Indian wars were periodically brought in for treatment or convalescence. Many ambitious soldiers with battle experience wanted to go on fighting after the end of the Mexican War, and found the opportunity to do so in various wars with the Indians: the Sioux War, the Apache Wars, the Cayuse War, the Utah War, and many other wars long before Custer's Last Stand. And the casualties kept dribbling in. It has been calculated that 15,000 soldiers lost their lives while killing 45,000 Indians. Mary Jane was a tender-hearted person, and she was always deeply moved by what she saw and by stories she heard of killing and maiming on the battlefield, for

267

whatever cause. She was delighted when her husband did what she told him to do: he resigned from the Army to go to work for her family's real-estate business in Chicago and to develop the social and political contacts in Louisville that stood him in such good stead later in life. /2

Although Buckner maintained an administrative position with the rank of Colonel in the State Militia, there was, for a time, relative peace and prosperity in the life of Simon Bolivar Buckner and his household.

Then something happened.

The Civil War broke out. The Buckners were not sure whether to zig or to zag. They would have liked to remain neutral, as indeed Kentucky officially tried to do, with its Governor leaning to the South and its Legislature leaning to the North. Like the rest of the state, they were torn by opposing forces pulling in two directions. Bolivar was torn between Southern sympathies stemming from his Virginia forebears on the one hand, and on the other hand his Illinois real estate business and Chicago in-law connections clearly on the side of the North. Mary Jane was torn between her Southern sympathies and her Northern roots. She "knew" from her studies and her Virginia friends that the eleven Confederate States had even more right to secede in 1860 and 1861 than did the eleven states that seceded in 1787. /3

Transcending all her seething emotions, and her sympathy for this side or that side, was her hatred of war.

/2 After the Civil War, Buckner became a State Representative and ultimately Governor of Kentucky.

She felt the South was "more right" than the North. Furthermore, after the early rout of the Northern forces at Bull Run, or Manassas, she believed the South would win the war in short order. Accordingly she told her husband to reject Lincoln's offer of a command in the Union Army and to join the Confederacy, just as Robert E. Lee had done a few weeks earlier. Thereupon the 38-year-old Buckner received a commission as a General in the army of the CSA -- the Confederate States of America -- and was given command of the Central Kentucky Division at Bowling Green, part of Major General Albert Sidney Johnston's Western Army of Kentucky and Tennessee. Faithful Mary Jane was distressed and distraught, and also quite worried, as she foresaw escalation of the violence of the war, and accordingly accompanied her husband to Bowling Green, where he took command of his division.

For a time there was little action in that area until suddenly, on the 4th of February, 1862, General Grant convened his troops from throughout the Southern Illinois Command and began loading them onto a series of flat-bottom river boats in Cairo, at the confluence of the Mississippi and Ohio Rivers. Escorted by several "ironclad" gunboats, they steamed up the Ohio River and into the Tennessee River, where they joined forces with

/3 The "Articles of Confederation and Perpetual Union" were adopted by the thirteen colonies in 1781 and created "the United States." When eleven states seceded in 1789 "in order to form a more perfect union," there were only two states remaining in the original United States. Rhode Island and North Carolina were left for many months as an independent two-state nation unto themselves.

269

additional troops Grant had sent overland. Their aim was to capture Fort Henry, located at a strategic bend of the river, where it controlled boat traffic and commerce covering a vast portion of the Confederacy. Grant was able to capture the fort on February 9 with little difficulty, for it had been poorly built and was badly located in a low marshy area. Flood waters from the rising Tennessee River had recently washed over the entrenchments, rendering most of the defending cannons inoperative or ineffective. The weakly held fort could barely offer token resistance. Grant was able to take possession quickly with a minimum of casualties. Fortunately the 3,000 or so CSA troops from the garrison had withdrawn and regrouped within the larger and more redoubtable muniments of Fort Donelson, twelve miles away, which guarded the mouth of another important river, the Cumberland. Fort Donelson would doubtless be Grant's next target.

Gen. A.S. Johnston, CSA Commander of the Western Army, realized the importance of Fort Donelson and had tried unsuccessfully to get General P.T.G. Beauregard to take command there. Beauregard had declined, citing a throat problem, leaving only three less competent generals for Johnston to rely on, namely Gen. John B. Floyd, Gen. Gideon J. Pillow, and Gen. Bushrod Johnson. Floyd, the senior of the three, was a politician with little or no military experience. As former Secretary of War in Buchanan's cabinet, he was under indictment for scandal and corruption and was terrified at the thought of being captured and facing a Federal court of law. Pillow, a lawyer and successful land speculator but an incompetent general, was also avoiding court charges in the North stemming from insubordination and an on-going feud with General

Winfield Scott dating from the Mexican War. General Johnson, a college professor of mathematics, was the man responsible for the disastrous choice of the indefensible marshy location for building Fort Henry nine months earlier. All three generals held different opinions, and they argued, passing command responsibilities back and forth, blaming each other for their indecision and ineptitude.

That is when Gen. A.S. Johnston sent Buckner to Fort Donelson to support and help coordinate the efforts of the other three generals, who could never agree on anything. This time Mary Jane went right along with her husband, just as "batmen," or personal servants, including slaves, often accompanied senior officers on both sides in those hectic days.

As the situation became more tense, the three factious generals could not agree on whether to attack Grant's force of 25,000 men with their 17,000, or to dig in and await assault in a defensive position. They chose the latter (perhaps because it required no positive decision to do so). Even then, when Grant's forces began to surround the redoubt, they could not agree on whether to stand and give battle or to try to evacuate. They decided to stay, but again, shortly later, they still could not agree on whether to fight or surrender when Grant's encircling cordon was complete and escape would have been more difficult than ever.

Now dutiful Mary Jane Buckner, who had come right along to give her husband encouragement and help with the ubiquitous wounded soldiers, knew something about war and the horrors of war. Although there had been but little fighting at Fort Henry and hence few casualties, several dozen wounded and mangled soldiers had been brought over to Fort Donelson. She was also upset having recently received news of her own dear brother's death in Missouri at the battle of Springfield in August. He had just graduated from West Point the previous June.

Now, here at Fort Donelson, fierce fighting promptly began, and in just two days there were almost 1,000 killed and 3,000 wounded, counting both sides. Mary Jane felt that, with Grant's forces surrounding Fort Donelson and squeezing tighter and tighter, she could foresee which way this battle was going, and perhaps which way the war would go too. The North was bound to win. She had been wrong before -- she realized that now. But when the other generals, Floyd and Pillow and Johnson, in shame and disgrace, turned command over to Buckner and slipped away in darkness to save their own skins, she knew what she had to do. She told Buckner he must surrender to avoid any more unnecessary bloodshed. Buckner wanted to fight on, but he knew his wife was usually right.

Bolivar Buckner agreed to ask Grant for surrender terms. Grant of course was his old friend and Army buddy from Mexican War days, and furthermore, once when Grant was in financial difficulties just a few years ago, Buckner had helped him out. He knew Grant would remember the favor and would propound generous terms if he offered to surrender the fort. Buckner was so confident of Grant's friendship and chivalry that he expected him to allow him and his men to peacefully evacuate and turn the fort over, unscathed, without further bloodshed. Or at worst be counted as prisoners and released under the oath of parole. To convince Grant of his sincerity and good will, Buckner gave orders to his troops that no one was to try to escape Grant's impervious encircling cordon, and even went so far as to post his own guards to prevent any such escape attempts.

There was one famous conscientious objector to this plan, namely Lt. Col. Nathan Bedford Forrest, who was in command of a battalion of horse cavalry assigned to support the Fort Donelson garrison. This insubordinate officer urged Buckner to try to break out, and brazenly told him that he was crazy to stay there and capitulate. Buckner was somewhat annoyed but unmoved. Forrest thereupon contumaciously announced, "I did not come here to surrender my command," and with that he withdrew with all his men, boldly disregarding Buckner's orders as he rode off into the night. He was successful. He and his men were able to force their way out of the cordon and lived to fight another day -- many more days -- actually having made an opening that 14,000 more of Buckner's men could also have used to escape had they been on their toes.

But Buckner remained. The next day, February 18, 1862, he sent a message to Grant requesting surrender terms, confident that his old friend Ulysses would be generous.

However, he was mistaken.

The Grant of today was not the Grant of old whom Buckner had once known. Grant was no longer a beggar, and was enjoying his power and growing stature in the Army that he felt had treated him badly when he was a junior officer seven or eight years earlier. He was riding high and was not about to turn soft now, friend or no friend. Furthermore, he had always held an unspoken grudge that had been festering in his heart for thirteen years. Buckner had embarrassed him and shamed him by climbing to the top of Mount Popocatepetl and then crowing about it when Grant's gout was hurting too much for him to continue all the way. Grant never told anyone that story, but he never forgot it either. Now, let Buckner come obsecrating and begging to him all he wants and see what he gets. It will serve him right.

Grant sent a simple reply to Buckner: "Unconditional surrender."

The phrase was to live in history for decades to come. "Nothing but Unconditional Surrender." Buckner couldn't believe his eyes. His old friend wouldn't do this to him. There must be some mistake. Buckner pleaded for some consideration.

"No way," came back the answer from Ulysses S. Grant. "Unconditional surrender -- immediate and unconditional surrender."

At that point the statistics of the Fort Donelson affair looked like this:

	Union Forces	Confederate Forces
Total forces	25,000	17,000
Killed	507	327
Wounded	1,976	1,127

If you were to stop there and ask yourself which side was winning, you might have said the South was doing pretty well, as indeed it was, with the ratio of killed and wounded being almost two to one in its favor. But the statistics did not stop there, and the next two lines tell the true tale; they looked like this:

Captured	208	12,392
Total losses	2,691	13,846

General Grant, elated by the results of his strategy, promptly sent Lincoln a telegram jubilantly announcing his victory. The capture of Fort Donelson, and especially the splendid enemy army almost unscathed, was the first great step in the winning of the War for the North. The script was now written. It was emulated the next year at Vicksburg when General John C. Pemberton followed Buckner's lead and ignominiously surrendered 29,495 more troops, 172 cannons, and almost 50,000 rifles to the Union forces after suffering 9,091 casualties compared to 10,142 by the Union side.

The prisoners from Fort Donelson, including General Buckner himself, were sent to Northern prison camps, such as Camp Chase Ohio, Fort Lafayette New York, Fort McHenry Maryland, and Fort Warren Massachusetts. (The notorious death camps at Douglas Illinois and Elmira New York were constructed later, especially built for prisoners.) Buckner expected to be paroled and must have been quite surprised to find himself imprisoned at Fort Warren, on tiny Georges Island near the entrance to Boston harbor, where he was punished by being placed in solitary confinement for the next five months. /4 His wife, Mary Jane, now in great distress, followed her husband's trail to Boston, stopping only briefly along the way to see a few friends and family for support and encouragement. On August 15, 1862, after almost half a year in solitary, Buckner was freed from prison in a clandestine exchange involving the release of Union General George A. McCall, who had been captured at Frayser's Farm in June and was being held in Libby Prison, Richmond. The exchange of prisoners was an illegal arrangement that had not been sanctioned by Lincoln's high command, which officially opposed prisoner exchange. Indeed, Edwin M. Stanton, Lincoln's Secretary of War, had given specific orders to Lt. Col. Justin Dimick, the Fort Warren Prison Commander, forbidding the release or exchange of any Confederate prisoners, including General Buckner, because he and Lincoln felt that an exchange would give the South, with its smaller army, a relative advantage.

/4 The Federal Prison at Fort Warren also held over 100 members of the Maryland State Legislature and other elected civil officials and political prisoners who were believed to be, or were even suspected of being, Southern sympathizers.

Mary Jane threw her arms about her dear husband, succored him, and in due course nursed him back to health. "I am so sorry, my Darling," she said. "I never should have told you to surrender to General Grant at Fort Donelson."

Before long, when he had regained his strength, Buckner returned to service with the CSA, this time with a promotion to Major General. Mary Jane later learned more about the frightful conditions in the prisoner-of-war camps both North and South, but especially in the North, where winter weather conditions were severe and prison authorities were said to be equally severe, or at best indifferent. Of the 12,000 prisoners from Fort Donelson, it was estimated that over 2,400 died in the following months, from exposure, undernourishment, lack of clothing, and disease in the camps. /5 She also realized that Fort Donelson was a major reason that the North ultimately emerged victorious. The 12,000 troops and weapons lost to Grant at Fort Donelson, plus the 30,000 lost at Vicksburg because Pemberton followed Buckner's lead, if kept alive, healthy, and well equipped, would have totaled 42,000 well-armed troops, enough to turn the tide of the War the other way.

From time to time, in the months and years to come, poor Mary Jane, wracked by remorse and contrition, relived and pondered her part in this. As she got older she would

---

/5 The death rate of the Confederate prisoners taken at Fort Donelson who died in Northern prison camps exceeded the death rate of Nathan Forrest's Confederate soldiers who avoided capture and fought on for three more years.

repeatedly say to her husband, "I am so sorry, my Darling. I never should have told you to surrender to Ulysses at Fort Donelson. I'm terribly sorry. I really am...

..   "Why did you listen to me?"

THE END

The Certificate

María Propelrendl was a good girl, but she was born and raised in the Old County, where things were different. She was especially good when she was very young. When she was three years old she didn't know anything about boys at all. Her only sibling at that time, Jeblinka, was six years older than María and was a girl, and her little brother hadn't been born yet. María, or Maya as her sister Jeblinka called her, obeyed her parents -- quite often. For instance, after she put the turtle in her parents' bed -- just for fun -- after she did that, they told her never to do it again, and she never did do it again.

What Maya really liked to do was hold hands. The little family always held hands in a circle when they blessed the meal at the supper table. Maya liked having Jeblinka hold her hand when she was learning to walk, and later it was nice when they crossed the street together. Maya liked that. She liked holding hands. Hands are wonderful things: they are the connection with a person you care for; they are the gateway into another person's soul; they are things that are fun to hold when they have sticky jam or mud on them, or even when they are spanking clean and have no jam or anything on them at all.

When Maya's little brother Zebulon came along -- she called him Zeb -- when Zebulon came along Maya was delighted to find that he had hands too, and used to hold hands with the baby almost as soon as his eyes were open.

279

She played with his tiny fingers, put marbles or toothpicks into his hands, and watched him giggle with joy, then cry with frustration when she took them away from him. When he cried she would hold his hand again and sometimes that was enough to shut him up.

Yes, hands are wonderful things for holding and playing with.

When Maya was old enough to go to school, she found a lot more hands she could hold. Sometimes the teacher would let her hold *her* hand, and Maya held hands with the other girls when they played ring-around-the-rosie, and crack-the-whip, and of course when crossing the street or practicing fire drill. It was also fun clapping hands or giving each other high fives when the school principal finished talking at morning assembly, or when they were allowed to play patty-cake at recess.

Hands were more fun to play with than anything else ever created, hands down.

When Maya was twelve or thirteen she noticed that boys had hands too, and not just her little brother, who was eight years old by then and had a pretty strong grip. She was proud of him and still liked to hold hands with him a lot, as well as boss him around and tell him what to do, but about that time she started holding hands with other boys too. The boys her own age were mostly too young or didn't care to hold hands with girls, but she found that boys who were a little older, sixteen or seventeen, didn't mind holding hands at all, and even seemed to like it, and some of them were pretty good at it.

By then her sister Jeblinka was nineteen and was happily married to her cousin Zekiel. So Zeke was Maya's cousin also, and he would often hold hands with her when she wanted him to, and he was quite good at it too. Zeke was the nephew of Dr. Zoltan B. Himmelfarb, the village doctor. Jeblinka had married well, as Himmelfarb was the richest man in town and had no children. Dr. Himmelfarb was 47 years old but had never married because he could never find a woman who met both his standards and his taste. Some of the women he knew had fine brains, and some of the women he knew had fine bodies, but none, it seemed, had both, as Himmelfarb saw it.

Zeke and Jeblinka were married young because that was the tradition in the Propelrendl family. Maya's mother had gotten married young too, back even before Jeblinka was born. According to the old traditions, you were supposed to be married before you knew much and were still too young for anything to happen that could lead you astray or sully your reputation. All of Maya's female relatives married young while they still had good reputations -- before the gossip columnists and quidnuncs could find anything scandalous to say about them. That is one good thing that you can say for old traditions -- they sometimes helped keep your name out of the gossip columns.

Maya kept on holding hands almost every chance she got, right through her school years and her teen years until she was nineteen. And then her mother thought it was time to find her a husband before she learned too much and ran the risk of getting into trouble.

But Maya was already in trouble. She didn't know it, and her mother didn't know it, but Maya was already getting a reputation. Now some reputation might be a good thing, such as the reputation of a famous general or ballet dancer, but the reputation that Maya was getting was the other kind, like notoriety. Hard as it is to believe, some of the shriveled-up old biddies in that little village, and other scandal-mongers, whether they had eligible sons or not, started gossiping about Maya's "behaviour." Maya had been seen publicly holding hands with boys on more than one occasion. To Maya, holding hands was part of living life, like eating and breathing and going to the bathroom. But that's not the way the vicious village tongues saw it. Anyone who would hold hands as promiscuously as Maya did must be tainted goods. In a traditional society like this, all proper marriages were arranged affairs, but when Maya's mother, Rackabel, inquired through her friends and acquaintances for suitable candidates for marriage -- young men that is -- she got cold shoulders at every turn. Maya couldn't possibly be a virgin after holding so many hands over the years.

Rackabel was incensed. She vociferously attacked anyone who asserted or even intimated that her Maya was not white-driven snow, purity incarnate. People began to laugh at her, and say things like, "The lady doth protest too much." None of them would believe Rackabel's forceful asseverations and vituperations, and she could find no mothers of eligible young men who would talk to her or even look at her.

She had to do something, but what? She wracked her brains and worried herself sick for weeks. Finally the solution came to her: Dr. Himmelfarb! He must be the answer. Himmelfarb was the village doctor, the GP, the ER, the OR, the EENT, the midwife, the PDQ, and the GYN all rolled into one.

So she took Maya -- took her in hand, as it were -- to see Dr. Himmelfarb, who in fact had delivered Maya into this world some years before, back when she was a baby.

"I want a certificate," Rackabel declared.

"Certificate?"

"Yes, a certificate."

"What kind of a certificate?"

"A certificate of purity," she said delicately but firmly.

"Purity? I don't understand."

Rackabel dropped her voice: "Virginity," she said to the stupid man. "We want a certificate of Maya's virginity. We'll pay you whatever it costs."

This sounded like some easy change for the good Doctor -- not only an interesting change of routine but also some jingling change in his pocket. Himmelfarb already had plenty of money but, like many other rich people, he was always glad to have a little more. So he agreed. He named his price and told Maya to go home and get a good night's sleep and take a good bath in the morning and come back to the clinic at ten o'clock for the examination.

It all worked out fine, just as Rackabel had envisioned and planned. Dr. Himmelfarb provided the certificate, had it notarized, and turned it over to Rackabel the same afternoon. Rackabel was delighted. She had the certificate framed in white oak with shatter-proof glass. "Now let them cast aspersions on my daughter or imply that she is impure," she thought. She proudly began again to make the rounds of all her old friends, especially those with nubile young sons or nephews, irrefutably proving what she had been claiming all along. Her daughter was a Certified Virgin, driven only by the pure white snow. She had them this time -- she thought.

They laughed at her. "I wonder how much she had to pay old Himmelfart for that!" they jeered. They all seemed to believe Maya was hiding something -- probably some serious sinning -- to have to go to such lengths to claim she was a virgin. No one took her seriously or believed her. The village mothers closed their doors on Rackabel's efforts to find a husband for Maya.

Then one day some astonishing news swept through the the little town. The news won a front-page spot in *The Village Vision*, the local weekly newspaper, although it was tainted by the bitter tongue of the Society Editor. The owner of the sharp tongue and sharper pen was a partially shriveled spinster named Molly Majoud. Molly was an orphan, so she had no parents to arrange a marriage for her, but undaunted, back when she was only 31 years old, she had spotted the up-and-coming young Himmelfarb, then a handsome unmarried 26-year-old intern, and decided she would fall in love with him if he could only give her half a chance. But he couldn't. He gave her an exciting little fling, but that's all. Then he promptly forgot it, but she didn't. Her buck teeth and acerbic personality were too much for the young doctor and fell short of his aforementioned high standards. He would rather go it alone. Maggie never forgot the brush-off and was now taking this final opportunity to squeeze a few bitter grapes:

VILLAGE DOCTOR WEDS LOCAL GIRL

Dr. Zoltan Himmelfarb, the richest man in town, was married Saturday at a lightly attended quasi-religious ceremony at the Hagia Triada Church. The bride was apparently none other than Maria Propelrendl, a young women half his age who is well known for her many activities about town and throughout the local area. This Maria is said to be the daughter of Jawaharlal and Rackabel Propelrendl of this village. Dr. Himmelfarb has announced that the Himmelfarb Medical Clinic will be closed for two months while the couple are getting off somewhere to an undisclosed location other than St. Tropez to spend their honeymoon.

Dr. Himmelfarb used to be known as a man of discriminating taste. We all wish him well and presume he knows what he is getting into.

THE END

Epilogue

Of course, Dr. Zoltan Himmelfarb did know. And apparently he was quite pleased, for he and Maya lived happily ever after and had lots of children.

And all their children loved to hold hands, in spite of what the neighbors said.

THE FINAL END

285

Other works by Daniel Hoyt Daniels

VERSE TRANSLATIONS OF MOLIÈRE COMEDIES:
Volume One: DON JUAN AND OTHER PLAYS
   "The Imaginary Cuckold"
   "A Doctor in Spite of Himself"
   "Don Juan"
Volume Two: THE MISANTHROPE AND OTHER PLAYS
   "Love is the Best Doctor"
   "A School for Husbands"
   "The Misanthrope"
Volume Three: THE IMAGINARY INVALID AND OTHER PLAYS
   "George Dandin"
   "The Learnèd Ladies"
   "The Imaginary Invalid"

"BAKED ALASKA and Other SHORT SHORT STORIES"
BAKED ALASKA
HEADS I WIN, TAILS I WIN
STORMY NIGHT
GOOD NEWS
THE LIVE OAK
THE RABBIT
BITCHES ON THE BEACH
HELLO THERE
PLAYING IT COOL
MAKING ARRANGEMENTS
THAT'S OKAY
ANYTHING YOU WANT
GETTING EVEN
HASTA LA VISTA
IT WOULDN'T BE ADVISABLE
A NEW START
THE PRODIGAL CALF
A FEW MORE DAYS
LIKE I SAID, AN ORDINARY GUY
TURKEY IN THE STRAW
JOHN HARVARD FANTOMA
MY BROTHER-IN-LAW IS A JERK
THE MOUSTACHE
MONEY, MONEY, MONEY
THE WORLD OF ART
THE BEARD
BASTILLE DAY – PROVING A POINT
LOCKS OF GOLD
HYPOCRISY, ANYONE ?
YOU TOOK THE WORDS

Other works by Daniel Hoyt Daniels

"THIRTY OF THE BEST SHORT STORIES"

A SCOUNDREL, MY FATHER
SORRY, I'M BUSY
THUMBS UP
THE FAITHFUL WIFE
OH, DIDN'T YOU KNOW?
THE TELEGRAM
THE LAST WORD
DIVORCE OLD FRENCH STYLE
WHITE MAN IN A BLACK SKIN
A HALLOWE'EN GHOST STORY
TOOTHPASTE, ANYONE?
WITHOUT MY GLASSES
RUN, RUN !
THE SECRET
I DIDN'T KNOW
COLLEGE TUITION
THE GRUDGE
HORSES
I WASN'T QUITE ABLE
IT'S YOUR COW
THE DOUBLE AGENT
HAPPY THANKSGIVING
REWRITING HISTORY
HOLY COW
THE BEST OF TIMES
DO YOU THINK YOU CAN?
WHAT'S IN A NAME
UNCLE CHARLIE
PRETTY GOOD ENGLISH
THE ASTROLOGER AND THE KING

Other works by Daniel Hoyt Daniels

"SHORT STORIES GALORE"

PENNIES FROM HEAVEN
ONCE A BUTLER
THE ABUSED CHILD
KEEPING IT LEGAL
WAITING AWAY
A PROPER UPBRINGING
ALTRUISM -- LOVE OF LIFE
AFFAIR, ANYONE ?
THE DREAM
ALWAYS IN LOVE
YOU'LL LOVE IT
CHINESE CHESS
THE DIPLOMATIC WEIGHT-WATCHER
TENOR, ANYONE ?
AND SO HE DID
THE MILLIONAIRE
HARMONY
MÉNAGE À TROIS
DISAPPOINTMENT
THANKS FOR THE MEMORY
BEST FOOT FORWARD
ONCE A KING, or THE RIVALRY
OLDER WOMAN
DOUBLE TAKE
MOTHER TONGUE
COUNT YOUR BLESSINGS
THE SIXTY-SECOND WORKOUT
DON'T LET IT BOTHER YOU
I ASSURE YOU
THE BRAIN

Other works by Daniel Hoyt Daniels

"SHORT STORIES FOREVER"

BEFORE HE EVER DIED
THE ORACLE
THE YELLOW SCHOOL BUS
MAD
SORRY, NO SPANISH
THE PROMISE
ECUMENICAL
MY SISTER'S BUTLER
YES SIR, OFFICER!
THE DEBUTANTE
STORY TELLING
IF YOU SHOOT IT
I COULDN'T AFFORD IT
GETTING WARMER
REPENTANCE
NIKE
HOW DEGRADING
OH, ALL RIGHT
DOLORES
RETIRED
I'LL SHOW YOU!
WHERE DID WE COME FROM?
USE YOUR PHONE
ONE GOOD ONE
DISTANT RELATIVE
THE WINDOW
THE BALLAD OF GOOD NEWS
FRIENDSHIP
HAPPY FELLA
PAIRING THE VOTE

Other works by Daniel Hoyt Daniels

"GRAMMAR TODAY"
Comprising a few more Rules Ruge (Ferdinand E.Ruge)
would have espoused for proper English usage.

ABBREVIATIONS
ADJECTIVE USED AS ADVERB
AGREEMENT OF SUBJECT AND VERB
ALRIGHT -- ALL RIGHT
APPRAISE -- APPRISE
COLLECTIVE NOUNS
COMMAS ON PARENTHETICAL EXPRESSIONS
COMPARISON OF ADJECTIVES
COMPRISE -- CONSTITUTE
DANGLING PARTICIPLES AND GERUNDS
DEFINITE -- DEFINITIVE
EACH OTHER -- ONE ANOTHER
   BETWEEN -- AMONG
EXPECTATIONS -- GOALS AND OBJECTIVES
FALSE ELLIPSIS
FIGURATIVE SENSE
FORBID -- FORBADE
FURTHER -- FARTHER
GERUNDS -- USE OF THE POSSESSIVE WITH GERUNDS
HEALTHY -- HEALTHFUL
I -- ME
"IF" CLAUSES, SUBJUNCTIVE OR NOMINATIVE?
IMPACT -- AFFECT
IMPACT -- EFFECT
INCREDIBLE -- UNBELIEVABLE
INCREDULOUS -- INCREDIBLE
IN EXCESS OF
LAPSES OF LOGIC, AND STUPIDITIES
LESS -- FEWER
"LET'S" MEANS "LET US"
LIE AND LAY -- SIT AND SET
LIKE
LIKE -- AS IF, AS THOUGH
MYSELF -- ME, I
NOT HELP BUT
ONE OF THOSE WHO
OVERWORKED PREPOSITION
PARTICIPLES ENDING WITH -ING
PAST PERFECT TENSE -- PAST TENSE
PLUS -- FURTHERMORE
PREPOSITION ASSOCIATED WITH VERB -- LOSS OF
SOMEPLACE -- PLACE
SPECIAL PLURALS
SUBJUNCTIVE FALLING INTO DISUSE
THAT -- VERY
TRANSITIVE VERB REQUIRES OBJECT
TWO SUBORDINATE CLAUSES
UNCOUNTABLE NOUNS
UNDER -- LESS THAN
VERB OR NOUN? -- PRONUNCIATION
WARMER TEMPERATURES -- HIGHER TEMPERATURES
WHICH -- THAT
WHO -- WHOM
WITH REGARDS TO
WOULD -- WOULD